Machinist of Mana

★ BOOK 2 ★

MACHINIST OF MANA

★ BOOK 2 ★

WANDERING AGENT

To Sue
Who always showed me the way

All rights reserved. No part of this publication may be reproduced, stored in a retrieval system, or transmitted in any form or by any means electronic, mechanical, photocopying, recording, or otherwise without prior written permission from Podium Publishing.

This is a work of fiction. Names, characters, places, and incidents are either products of the author's imagination or used fictitiously. Any resemblance to actual events, locales, or persons, living, dead, or undead, is entirely coincidental.

Copyright © 2026 by Michael Robert Taylor

Cover design by Yanhong Lu

ISBN: 979-8-89539-876-0

Published in 2026 by Podium Publishing
www.podiumentertainment.com

Machinist of Mana

★ Book 2 ★

CHAPTER 1

★

CHANGE OF PLANS

I passed along the halls of my school, an academy for young knights. Outside young men sparred in one of the fields, others studied on the grass in the summer sun. Now well into my second year of school, I had today off, and it was time to relax and kick back.

Months had passed since our last encounter, and still my green-skinned enemies hadn't made themselves known again. Some things of minor note happened, of course, but nothing as serious as they could have been. That was good. My teachers were still none too pleased with me finding trouble while away from school.

At one point there was a request from the local authorities that I consult with them on some firearm designs I'd provided. That was easy enough, and I quickly found solutions to the problems they were having. It was clear that they didn't have the right experts for the adjustments they were trying to make to my designs, so I was just the person they needed, even if I was an amateur by my own estimation. A few notes here and there about adjusting size, pressure, and general layout and they quickly had something they could use. I still tried to push for everything to be massively overbuilt, because if a gun was too thick in certain areas, it would be heavy, but too thin and it could result in catastrophic failure.

Overall, things were going well. In fact, the only thing at all that was going wrong was the letter I'd received just this morning. My parents had written me a letter, in a flowery explanation that really could have been summed up in two sentences, and had told me that they would not be coming to the city during the winter this year. Instead, I was left to my own devices. That meant I would need to take over management of the house and staff; though the staff did most of that on their own.

On a happy note, this meant that I could check on my younger half-sister with impunity. My father has hidden her existence, and basically everyone thought I should have nothing to do with "servants" other than purely professional things. Even the few who knew of my father's indiscretion with one of our maids wanted me to stay at arm's length. I had other plans though. After all, it was a big brother's job to keep an eye out for his siblings, and one I wouldn't shirk.

"Oh, there you are," said Lucas, approaching me at speed.

I ducked under my best friend's arm. He'd attempted to pull me into a headlock. He was a good guy, but a bit of a fanatic about training.

"Good morning, Lucas," I said without missing a beat. "How are things?"

"Excellent! The sun is shining, the breeze is blowing, and it's time to train!"

"Don't you get enough from the headmaster? He has me doing session after session now, and I know you're on a similar schedule."

"Never enough, my friend, never enough. So, you, me, arena."

"Can't right now, unfortunately. I've got business in the city." I passed him the note, earning a frown.

"Are they even letting you into the city on off days?"

"Eh, it's been long enough since the last incident that they're loosening the restrictions, and it's not like I'll be alone."

My reputation for chaos had spread, much to my chagrin. None of it was my fault, of course, or at least most of it wasn't. The simple fact of the matter was that the city's goblin problem was still in full swing, even if they'd failed to find the little buggers. There weren't even any actual reports of them, so I could tell they weren't meeting with success in dislodging the green menace beneath the streets.

Honestly, I didn't know if the local authorities could handle the goblins, and I couldn't do too much to help them. The fact was that their leader was a centuries-old biomancing madman from my former world, and this led to some significant issues for anyone trying to dislodge them. Even if I could tell the local leaders, which I couldn't, and they believed me, which they wouldn't, I'm not sure it would've helped much.

"However are you going to catch up to me then? You know I'm beating you more and more by the week."

"Don't know that I will, Lucas, and that's all right," I said. "You'll never be the shot or machine worker I am."

He looked at me almost pained, but what was there to do? I liked the fencing matches we had, to be sure, but I wasn't obsessed like he was. He was well on his way to becoming a master of the art, while I fell behind constantly. Originally, he and I had been evenly matched; but he was right. He was pulling ahead slowly but steadily.

"You could," he countered. "You've got a gift for it."

"No, I trained all through childhood. Heck, I'm still training far more than nearly anyone except you now, but . . ." I wasn't having the same improvements. Progress, sure, but not like he was having.

"Fine, but you'd better be putting your all into your weapons."

I simply smiled. Perhaps I didn't have either his gift or drive for swordplay, but when it came to other things I was progressing nicely. Hidden amongst my papers and things were blueprints, and the beginning parts of some truly amazing weapons, ones that suited me far better than blades, and would work for others too. Soon, so very soon, we'd have a new era in this world, one in which I'd be at the forefront. I had things to do today, I slipped into a carriage and soon found myself traveling in a familiar direction. Trees and fields gave way in short order to walls of stone and brick, the roads shrinking to fit between the rising buildings. Street by street we moved until a house I'd come and gone from for most of my life rose before me once more.

Departing from my conveyance, I strolled up to the front door and opened it. Unlike the normal homecoming my family had once a year, the staff were not lined up and ready to greet me. In fact, I was alone in the entry, looking around with a light smile at the decorations. I never did tire of the stylistic art mother had hung here.

While I was staring at one particularly lovely painting of a sunrise over a snowy mountain, I heard a call from behind me.

"Excuse me, sir," the maid who'd stumbled upon me began. "What exactly..." She was clearly displeased someone had just waltzed right into the house without so much as knocking. When she saw my face she snapped back. "Apologies, m'lord. I didn't know you were coming by today. Can I be of any assistance?"

Sadly, I'd scared the poor girl. She'd thought I was some intruder to be chased off, and had even begun to raise her voice, which was good. However, with the distinctions in society and the strict discipline some people kept, she might well expect to be punished for doing so to a member of the family she worked for. There were people like that, but not being a complete bastard, I wasn't one of them.

"Ah, my apologies for that," I said in a soft, relaxed tone. "I didn't quite have time to send word ahead. Would you be so kind as to find Mrs. Rider and let her know I'd like a word?" I asked in a soft, relaxed tone.

"Of-of course, right away." She turned on her heel and fled.

Was I really that intimidating? I tried my best to be a decent man to everyone I met, but then again, I supposed the house staff didn't interact with me all that much. Shaking my head, I went back to my contemplation, this time on a cityscape of somewhere I'd never been.

CHAPTER 2

✶

PAPERWORK AND ENCOURAGEMENT

I did not aim to cause the staff stress, but I did so with aplomb. Mrs. Rider, the housekeeper for this particular home, soon found me where the maid had. She looked a bit surprised but was well composed. She looked at me, and at the small bag the coach had left, before speaking.

"Lord Percival, I wasn't expecting you at all. Was there some issue?" she asked with a rush.

"Not a particular one," I replied. "Did you get a letter from my parents?"

"No, I can't say I've had one in the last few days, but that's hardly odd."

Luckily, I'd brought the one they'd sent to me, which I handed over to her. Her brow creased a bit as she read it, sighing when she reached the end.

"Indeed. While I'm not in a rush today, I was hoping you might be able to go over the expenses with me early. I imagine it will be a tribulation based on how Mother regards them and would prefer to get started early."

My mother might not manage the day-to-day functions, but the expenditures were ultimately part of her responsibilities. Unlike my father, who would work with those outside the home to bring in money, she made sure it was all going where it was supposed to—checking finances, receipts, and the like to see that we weren't being swindled and that everything was in its place. I knew she received monthly reports from the city house, but she went into much more detail for several days every winter to check the books.

"That's no problem, but I'm afraid we don't have any of the upstairs offices open right now. Would it be acceptable to use mine?"

"Certainly."

Mrs. Rider's office was a small room near the female staff's dormitories. There were a number of the more expensive supplies for the house as well as bookcases of paperwork everywhere. With only a pair of seats to be had, she tried to let me use the one behind her desk, but I insisted on a smaller stool instead. After all, I was the guest here.

For most of the first day I worked alone, the housekeeper having other things to do. Even during downtime she still had over a dozen staff to manage and a house to run. I bent over the books, checking receipts and records.

"I think the butcher is overcharging," I told her when she finally returned. It wasn't much, but the costs were above what they ought to be. Only a few months into this year's work, and I could see that already.

"Oh, I agree, and I have told your mother as much, but she wants to keep with him. There've been reports of a few of the others in town serving less than stellar meats, sometimes even different animals than they've advertised."

"That's fair." If they both knew, then I'd leave it to them. "How about the staff? How are they doing?"

"Well enough. We've hired a new boy to help with the coaches, as the old one is now being trained as a footman. He's not up to snuff yet, but should be by the time winter rolls around." I appreciated her candor. Training was important, and while he needed to be ready for winter, if he wasn't, he simply wasn't.

"Good, and the maids?" I asked, hoping to get some news on my little sister.

"Doing well, anything in particular you're worried about?"

"No, but I'd like to have a word with the staff at some point individually if that's well and good. See if there are any concerns they have that I need to address."

Mrs. Rider gave me a kindly smile, seemingly pleased that I was so interested in the well-being of the people working for me. In this world such concern was not a given; though, on Earth many managers hadn't cared for their workers either. However, I felt that it was important to know such things, and to fix them before they became problems. Though, honestly, I really was mostly concerned about one maid in particular.

"I'll see to it," she said, nodding happily.

Satisfied that I'd gotten at least some of the housework done, I retired to my private workshop. There was dust everywhere, as it wasn't somewhere I wanted any of the staff to go, but I had a few things I wanted placed here. My previous weapon had been an oversized revolver, but my next one, oh it would be something a bit more energetic.

In my absence the materials and machines I'd received from the duke had been delivered, mostly piled beside the door. These I quickly moved to the places I thought they'd fit best and began working.

My first attempt at making a piece of brass was lackluster, taking longer than I'd like and the dimensions were slightly off. For some applications that would be fine, but not for this one. I scrapped it and began again. Soon I'd found a rhythm, and it wasn't until a knock came from behind me that I looked away from my labors.

"Lord Percival, will you be staying for dinner?" It was Kaylee who'd been sent to check on me, and she stood there in the doorway, looking inside.

"Hmm? Oh, hello there, Kaylee," I replied. "Ah, no, but it is getting late, isn't it? Thank you for letting me know." I smiled a bit despite myself. She was still the same cute little sister she'd always been.

"Of course, sir. Do you need anything else?"

"No, no I'm quite well. How are you, by the way? It's been some time since we've spoken."

"I'm well, sir, quite well." I had to restrain myself from telling her not to be so formal.

"Excellent, and your magic? Still practicing?" I asked.

"Oh, yes; though I can't do much more than make a small fire. Mrs. Rider is happy to let me use it to light the fireplaces and the ovens in the morning. So I'm getting some use of it at least."

"Well, keep at it, and I'm sure things will improve for you. And, if you ever want to charge some items, let me know. I'm sure I can find something for you," I said, knowing that I could give her a better rate than anyone else would.

"Thank you, my lord," she answered with a shy smile.

"Look at the time. I must be off if I'm to return to the school before curfew. My thanks again for stirring me, and do be well."

As I rushed off to return to school I wondered what she'd been thinking. Did she know what I knew? Or did she think I was some odd rich boy, or perhaps inappropriately interested in her, or that perhaps it was just our shared connection to her mother and my childhood nanny? At some point I'd have to find a way to tell her the truth, but I knew neither how nor when would be the right time to do such a thing.

CHAPTER 3

NOT MY FAULT

School was, well, school, even if a number of the subjects were different in this life, it remained much the same as my previous life. Sure, there were no computers to type up our reports and essays, and sure, we had much more gym, and it was significantly more violent, but boys were boys regardless of the time period or place. The administration was always trying, and failing, to enforce discipline, the students always determined to get into any manner of trouble.

While I had been involved in a minor rebellion on my first day of school, it wasn't my turn today; it was Simon's. One of my closer friends in this institution of education, the boy had been caught in some shenanigans, and for some reason I'd been brought in with him. There was a message for me at lunch informing me I was to come to the headmaster's office, nothing more.

"Why is it always you who ends up in my office?" our headmaster said, looking down at me.

"Honestly, sir, I've no idea why I'm here."

"He had nothing to do with it, sir," Simon protested.

"You two expect me to believe that?" He leaned over his desk, glaring.

"Sir," I told him, my hackles raising. "We've met. When have you known me to lie? If I'd done something I thought you'd be this angry over, I'd just tell you."

He narrowed his eyes even more, picking up a small box and putting it on the desk between us. With a frown I opened it, and inside I found something most unexpected. The pieces were small and complex, more complex than most people worked with, but they weren't mine. This wasn't machined, but rather magically constructed, and while I could see clearly that they moved, I didn't know what they did. There were even a pair of highly polished gems.

"What are they?" I asked.

"Pieces of a golem, headmaster," Simon responded. "Percival had nothing to do with this; it was all me."

"You? Young Simon, a skilled enough student you may be, but I've seen enough over the years to know that you're not good enough to design these. I'd even doubt you could come up with the instructions to make them on your own."

That was why I'd been brought in then. The headmaster thought I had helped him create a golem; though this one would only be about the size of my palm. I hadn't, of course. They were rare things; hard to design, harder to control. Magically speaking, they were among the most complex of projects.

"Ah . . . I didn't do it either. The designs and instructions came from a book. My father designed these; they're supposed to be a toy. He never made any, but there's this girl, and I thought . . ."

"That you would make a highly banned item in my school?" the older man growled.

It was true. There were laws, lots of them, about magical items. Certain wards were disallowed, too dangerous to the public, certain functions completely banned for even study. Golems themselves were highly, highly regulated, to the point that I'd never even seen one. Most of the designs were showpieces, kept to prove that it could be done, like war engines, useful for generations of people.

The law used to be a lot looser, a lot more permissive on what people could make, but there'd been incidents. As both magical theory and technology increased, so too had the dangers of certain spells; ideas that wouldn't have been feasible in years past were now very possible. In the case of golems, there'd been a particularly bad incident where a security model had become confused about what it was to guard and from whom. Massive magically enhanced metal monsters were not simple to kill, and that one had required military intervention in the form of artillery bombardment. Golem construction had been highly regulated afterward.

"I'm sorry, sir, I didn't think—" Simon began.

"Clearly, golems don't either," the headmaster said, interrupting Simon. "That's the problem with them. A golem made to dig, digs; it doesn't care if there are people in the way, or buildings, or anything else. Even simple toys made to do things like run in circles can become dangerous if there's nothing to stop them, no proper protections. These things are banned for a reason, boy!" Then he turned to me. "Well, Percival, you at least have my apology. It seems that for once in the past two years you're actually not part of the mess I find on my desk."

"Thank you, sir," I said quickly, happy to be excused.

"Leave now while I decide what to do with your companion here."

It wasn't until dinnertime that I managed to find Simon again. I'd been worried when he missed our next class, but he was still here, just looking thoroughly tired.

"You all right there?" I asked, sliding in next to him at a table.

"Yes, I'm . . . well."

"What happened? Percival here wouldn't share the details," Lucas added, joining us. He may have been an upperclassman, but he still hung out with us every now and again. "Though, he did insist it wasn't his doing this time. What'd you do? Sneak naughty pictures into the school? Steal from a classroom?"

"I was trying to make something I shouldn't have, and he got dragged in because he's a troublemaker," Simon said, looking over to me. "Sorry about that, by the way."

"It's fine," I answered. "What I'm more interested in is how you planned to actually make it. That would imply you finished at least the first level of your core, wouldn't it?"

I knew the people in the class for making magical items this year, and Simon here wasn't one of them. How did he plan to make a golem if he couldn't even do that? No, if he was planning that, if he even went through the effort of making the parts, he had to have thought of that issue.

"Uh . . . don't share it around, but I got one years ago."

"What, how?" Lucas asked.

Simon seemed a bit taken aback. "Dad's a wizard, likes books and all that stuff. He taught me when he thought it was right. Reason I don't advertise is, well, it's kind of nerdy, isn't it?"

"Should I take that as a personal insult?" I asked lightly. I didn't think he meant it as one, but I didn't like his tone.

"No, I mean, you do amazing things with machines—guns and engines whatnot—not . . . toys and pretty lights. Does that make sense?"

"Only if you're willing to help me with a few projects," I asked with a smile.

"What do you have in mind?" Simon asked. Lucas just laughed.

CHAPTER 4

★

A PROPOSITION

I didn't care about Simon just because of golems. Sure, I could, in theory, come up with some great ideas of what to do with them but, more importantly, he had access to an actual core. One of those was illegal to have around. It was a tool of extreme danger. A golem was normal, something anyone could have, something anyone could use themselves.

Simon was also a friend though, so I wouldn't draw him into the worst of my ideas, but there were so many. Before we could do anything serious, I wanted to see some basics first. Everyone had their own way of doing things, and I wondered what his was.

"So, can you show me some of the things you've made?" I inquired when we'd made our way back to the dorm buildings.

"I can, but I'm surprised that you're not able to do it already. Is there a reason you've not fully built your first core yet?" he asked.

Cores came in three basic levels, and while the literature dithered on what each should be called, it was a simple progression. The first level, often called the apprentice core, would allow the most basic of enchantments and was what most people used. Then came the journeyman core, which was robust and constructed with more depth, allowing for far more to be done. Finally, there was the master core, which had extensive functions and was used by almost nobody due to the complexity at which one needed to work to make it function properly.

"No time," I responded.

"You've been working on that kind of thing for like a year though?"

"And it normally takes a year or more for that first level to be complete. Thing is I can't put the kind of time I need into building upon it."

"Why?"

"Have you seen my class schedule?" I laughed. It was well known among my friends that I hardly had free time for anything.

"All right then, but can't you buy anything you want? Your family is easily as wealthy as mine." That too was true, but it was true for almost everyone here.

"Hardly," I replied. "My parents give me an allowance, and custom-made pieces for my own enjoyment are not in the budget."

Almost everyone at our school was wealthy in some way or another. That was just part of being able to wield magic. There was an endless need for enchantments, for spellwork, for powerhouses in any industry. Even the staff at my home who had minor magics, like my sister, weren't poor, and probably never would be. Her income, and the income of anyone with such abilities, was several times what a non-magical person would make.

"And I'm assuming you don't bother to make your own money to supplement it either?" I did, but that was hardly his business, particularly because my money had come mostly from selling guns to the local government, or at least the plans for the weapons.

"Now, now, this is hardly the time to be speaking of such things. I just wanted to see what you can do."

"So you can use me," he griped.

I opened my mouth to respond, but closed it. He'd pointed it out too quickly for me to deny.

"My apologies, Simon. That was what I was doing, wasn't it? I was seeing what I wanted, not what you wanted."

"Well, you did get pulled into my mess, so I wasn't going to complain too much . . ."

Simon wasn't my closest friend, but he was still a friend, and I'd wronged him. That . . . hurt. I knew people like that in both of my lives, and I wanted to do better, be better. Too many people longed for a second chance like the one I'd gotten, a chance to live a life different from the one they'd had, a chance to fix the mistakes they'd made, and here I was taking it for granted. I stopped where I was, drifting off into thought.

"No, you're right to complain. I was being a proper fool. I'll agree that it was annoying for me to get pulled into your nonsense, but you don't owe me anything at all for it, do you? After all, nothing really came of it. That said, I'd still love to see your work, if you'll show me."

Simon didn't answer me at first, and then finally laughed and punched me in the shoulder.

"Ow!"

"Stop being serious," he said. "Come now, let's go."

Simon was feeling generous enough to show me some of his work, and honestly it wasn't all that impressive. Sure, everything was magic, but he wasn't doing much with it. There was a lamp, a heater for water, and a few other odds and ends that he'd made, but all were the simplest versions that could be made. There were no controls to change the intensity, no frills, barely an on/off control to them. Even if everything worked, they didn't work optimally, and they didn't do anything other than the most basic functions.

"So, what do you think?" he asked.

"I think if this is your work, you weren't ready for making a golem. Simon, I know you're better than all this. Even if you don't like this kind of thing, it's not something you should put away, or ignore."

"Well, everything works, does it not?" he griped.

"It could work better, which we both know. You were going to impress some girl with a fancy item, but what would have happened had she ever seen you using this?" I asked, poking his lamp to turn it on, then off. It was a simple cube, and frankly, ugly. All of his items were unbelievably ugly.

"That's true..."

With a smile, I made a proposition. "Maybe my eyes were getting a bit big for what I wanted, too, but I do have a proposal, if you're interested." At his raised eyebrow I continued. "Why don't we remake these? I could certainly use the practice, and between the two of us we have the skills to make much nicer things for you."

"And what are you getting out of this?" he asked.

"Practice, and seeing the process in action; though, I won't complain if you decide to make a few extras. I know plenty of theory, and I'm sure I can machine out a few nice outer shells for these, but I've never done it. Even the professors have only shown us the whole thing once or twice."

"All right, let's do it," he said with a smile.

CHAPTER 5

★

PREPPING FOR WORK

Simon and I had to wait a bit to really get to work, mostly because I was too busy to do much more than I already was. That said, I did give him a few tips on what he should look for in features and even loaned him a couple of my schoolbooks on programming. The latter would help for looking up commands and useful sequences but didn't really contain anything groundbreaking.

While he did that, I thought about some shell designs and how I'd go about making each of them, along with how I'd do what he should be doing—nothing too specific, just some basic notes. Even so, we had access to the shop in the school, and I was sure that we could come up with something quite nice. In fact, I had some ideas based on pieces from my previous world that I thought might go over well.

The evening before our day off we had time, so we went to see Professor Ruian.

"Good evening, Professor," I said as the two of us entered her office. "I was hoping that we might have you look over something."

"Hopefully not some attempt to make another weapon with my tools," she said with a frown. Apparently, what I'd done had gotten back to her.

"No, ma'am," I said. "I promise we won't be doing that."

"Or any other illegal items," she responded, pointedly looking at Simon.

"No, Professor," he said, looking a bit embarrassed.

"Hmm, what do you need then? Your work in my class has been acceptable, so I don't think we have any homework you'd need help with."

It was clear that she was suspicious, and that was fair. Each of us had caused this particular professor no small amount of trouble, and while I hadn't heard anything, I was sure that someone had given her a talking to about letting students do things like this. She'd caught Simon though, so there was that.

"Just looking at making a few small items, Professor," Simon said. "Would you be willing to look over things to make sure we didn't do anything wrong?" Simon passed her the runic sequences we'd written down, the codes for the items we were planning to make.

The professor took them without losing her scowl, and I worried. She'd been so friendly before, so full of joy. Had we taken that from her with our hijinks? I certainly hoped not. She was good at what she did, and making her lose her love of it certainly wasn't what I'd intended.

"These are . . . not bad. There's some room for improvement in the efficiency, and you need to add some limiters in a few places, but otherwise, not bad at all." She even made notes on the pages where we needed to improve them.

Looking over what she'd written, the reasoning was obvious. Simon hadn't added in upper limits to how much heat or light the items he was making could produce, and that was mildly dangerous. They couldn't really explode or anything, since they simply wouldn't be putting out that sort of energy, but they could burn things, or potentially hurt someone's eyes. It was something I should have thought of.

"Um . . . we were hoping to make these tomorrow, if you don't mind us using some of the equipment," Simon added as he, too, looked over the notes.

"We have a new policy that students are only allowed access to certain pieces of equipment under direct supervision of a member of staff, and you are fortunate that I will be here tomorrow afternoon. She wrote the hours she'd be in on a slip of paper and handed it to us. I'm sure you two understand why such a policy is necessary?"

"Yes, ma'am," we chorused.

A quick check on my part confirmed that the machine shop now had similar restrictions as well. I was surprised, but also relieved. I might be fairly safe to use those tools alone, but others certainly weren't as trained, and it would be a real shame if some kid got hurt. We also got lucky in that it would be open in the morning.

We met once more as the sun crested the horizon, spilling pale light over the countryside. It was beautiful, really, the pink stretching across the sky before fading into a pristine blue. There was not a cloud in sight, a perfect day. It was really a shame we'd be inside for most of it.

"You know, you never told me about this girl you were making the golem for," I said as we left the dorms. "Magical items are nice, but does she even have a way to power one?"

"She's a priestess," Simon said with a blush. "So that wouldn't be a problem. We met when I had to go for some healing—broken leg over the winter break."

I looked at him with raised eyebrows. All the boys at this school were physical magic users, and it took a significant amount of force to break one of our bones. Some of us could lift small cars if we were in the mood to, or move at superhuman speeds, so even the least durable of us was still quite difficult to injure.

"I'd rather not go into how," he demurred when he saw my look. "It's a bit embarrassing."

"All right, so you met her when you went to get healed and ended up courting?"

"Indeed," he replied. "She's so kind, and her face is like porcelain, surrounded by golden locks . . ." He looked off into the distance. "Add to that, she doesn't really have anything nice, other than a few formal outfits, so I wanted to make something special for her."

"Doesn't have anything nice? Goodness, a caster of any kind should be able to afford at least a few things."

"She lives at the temple for training, and they encourage a very . . . ascetic lifestyle. Not allowed to sell mana to anyone for things beyond needs and discouraged from buying fancy things. A gift would be fine, so I thought the little golem would be perfect." It was clear that he was trying to give her something to impress her.

"What magical items does she have? Maybe we can think of something."

"Oh, so far as I know, nothing. She said they issue small allowances for things like oil lamps and wood for heating . . ." he said, nearly stopping where he stood. "Oh, I'm a fool, aren't I?"

"At least you realize it," I teased, seeing that he now understood what he should have been doing.

"We'll need something pretty though. I'd hate to give her some ugly thing. Hope you don't mind me saying, but I'd like something different for her—something, oh I don't know, feminine."

"How about flowers?" I offered. I'd turned a few for decorations back on Earth. Tulips were easy, and with a bit of imagination, you could even make others. "I could make several of different metals, and we could make each like the items you're making for yourself."

"That wouldn't be too hard?" he asked.

"Not at all," I assured him. "We should even have enough metal in stock. It will be like giving her a bouquet, but useful."

"Yes, yes let us do that!" He was thrilled with the idea.

He was quite excited, and so was I, as we entered the shop. I breathed deep, the smell of oil and metal filling the air, the sun pouring through the windows. It was an absolutely perfect day, and the only way it could possibly improve was if I'd been able to do this partially outside, like when I used to work in my garage in my first life.

CHAPTER 6

MAGICAL ITEM CREATION

My hands tingled as the lathe spun to life. It didn't have the hum I was so used to from Earth, the gears being run by magic instead of an electric motor, but it did make a slight sighing noise. The machine was so quiet, nearly a whisper, a whisper of what it could do, what it could make. These were the tools of civilization, of the bringing of people from the medieval era to a modern one.

There was no doubt in my mind that the metal lathe had been the key, the absolute key to the industrial revolution, and that was true both here and back where I'd come from. The ability to make accurate machine parts for little money had changed the way the world worked. Perhaps there'd been some inklings of it in this world before, with the power of magic, but now the common man had access to it as well.

Simon had insisted that we make the parts for his love interest first, and I was happy to comply. The first would be a tulip which, as far as I could tell, existed here in exactly the same form as it had in my first world. The long cylinder started to spin, and I began my work.

We'd already cut out a cross section to form the petals, but I needed to bring things down, shape and alter, bit by tiny bit. Small slivers of metal pulled away as I worked the tools where they needed to sit, shaved by blades with careful precision. I lost myself as I worked, careful to prevent any overly sharp edges on the end product. Once the bud was complete, I finished out the stem. It would be a simple length, not quite a foot long, the brass polished to a brilliant shine. When the first flower was finished, I sat it to the side and began the next. A lot of flowers couldn't be made exactly, at least not with this tool, but several renditions of them could be made to work. It was a refreshing exercise, something different. So much of my work had to be exacting, pushed to the very limits of what I could make fit, measured and absolutely smooth. Not this though. This wasn't the artwork of perfect machines moving in ideal ways. No, this was a different art, one where flaws and organic curves and angles were not just acceptable, but ideal.

After my third piece, I turned to see Simon engrossed in what I'd been doing, and beside him Professor Turner, the metalworking teacher, looked pleased.

"Not a complex piece, but well done," he said as he examined my work. "And quite lovely. Would you mind if I used the design as an example for class? It's something the other students should be able to manage."

"No, sir, please feel free." After all, I wasn't the one who'd thought of the idea of turning flowers, though admittedly, most of the ones on Earth had been carved from wood rather than metal.

Once I was finished with all of the flowers, I began working on Simon's pieces. Well, those and several extras, because I wanted some as well. He was willing to make a few additional items without complaint because I was helping him, and I was going to take advantage of it. They'd all be shaped rather like small bowls or vases. Simple enough, small, and perfectly good for their purposes.

Honestly, when I'd first considered designs, I'd wanted to make them all look like adult toys, things nobody would recognize but would be humorous to me. Sadly though, someone had taken the time to make such things in the past, and so I had to abandon that plan, lest they be seen for what they were. This meant that I couldn't give Simon a wall of magical butt plugs to heat, cool, or light his room with. It was a sad day for humor everywhere. Even if I had the mind of an adult, I was bound and determined to maintain the humor of a child. If not, what was the point?

It took time, but time flew as I worked, and before I knew it, not only was most of the day gone, but I was done. One by one, my projects were lined up and placed along the counter. Simon was pleased, I was pleased, and the professor had decided at some point that we weren't causing trouble and left us alone. We could cause trouble now, but why break his trust? It was all well and good, all ready for the next step.

I cleaned up, making sure not to leave my workspace a mess. Shavings went into bins, and tools were double-checked that they were off and set correctly. There was a protocol for all of this, ways of working that would make it so that whoever came in next wouldn't have problems, and such things were important.

By the time everything was said and done, it was easily time for lunch, so the two of us took a break.

"I love these," Simon said, picking up one of the flowers I'd made, "and I'm sure Priscilla will too."

"Excellent, glad to hear it," I said, before taking a spoon to the hearty stew the school was serving.

"The professor's right—others might want them too."

"Then they can make them," I said. "It isn't hard." He laughed at that, shaking his head.

"No lady in your life that you'd want to make something for?"

I thought for a minute, then frowned. Rowena would probably love something I made, and she would be understandably peeved should she learn that I was making things for other girls and not her.

Was I sure that I wanted to end up with her? No, but I was absolutely sure that I didn't want trouble.

"I'll think of something else. Repeating the same thing for two girls would be a bit crass, wouldn't it?" As I spoke, I was spinning up plans in my head. "Don't suppose I could convince you to help me when the time comes?" I asked.

"Of course," Simon replied. "Though, you should really finish your own core."

"I know, I know, it's just scheduling." That was an excuse. He was right; doing so would strengthen me significantly.

When we finally finished, it was my turn to watch him work. None of the tools here were actually required for making an item into a magical one. That could be done manually, but they helped. They made sure that the central part of the item, its own core, so to speak, was well hidden within it and were good for applying quick finishing touches.

Every item had a core, just like people. In fact, they came from the maker themselves, a copying function from each person who had one. Unlike the creation of the human version, the item's was quick, rapidly assembled within whatever shell you made to contain it. The rune sequences—previously looking much like a written coding screen in the mental space, where they were laid out—snaked their way along the item in question. These could be hidden, jumbled in such a way that they became nonsense, but for something like what we were doing, there was no point.

Professor Ruian watched us like hawks the whole time. It was clear that she still had a pretty low opinion of our previous antics, but there was also a small smile when she saw the items we'd prepared for the process.

Even these weren't technically needed, since a magical item could be any shape desired. For the sake of efficiency, most of them were spheres, contained within other decorative pieces. Spheres were by far the most efficient shape, though nobody really knew why. Unfortunately, if you used one, it was only the sphere itself which functioned as the item. This was fine for most things and could be worked around with proper rune usage, but having the whole item itself be magical had other advantages. It was easier to charge such things, and they also simply shouted what they were, for appearances' sake.

Simon took his time. After all, this was a delicate process and not one that could be repeated if he failed. The first time a magical item was deemed complete would be the last, the runes locking themselves in and becoming unchangeable. It meant that if he screwed up even a little, there was no fixing it. We'd have to start again from scratch.

It took a couple of hours, but eventually Simon, too, finished his part. Unlike Professor Turner, who'd shown interest but quickly left us to ourselves, Professor Ruian stayed with us the whole time. She even inspected each construct when it was finished, testing it carefully to make sure it did what we said it did.

"Done," Simon finally declared, looking exhausted as he set down what should now be a lamp.

"Hmm," the teacher said, picking up the device and pumping a bit of mana into it.

The runes along the surface lit up as they absorbed her power, showing how much energy was in it. This was how people knew when to charge things, and this process even served as a useful metric for a difficult concept—the amount of mana in something.

"Very well," the professor finally declared. "Good work, boys. If only some of your classmates would show such creativity focused on positive results, we might well see a new era."

"Thank you, ma'am," we offered her in succession, and she shooed us off.

CHAPTER 7

DATE

I sat looking at the small box that I'd designed. It'd taken work from both Simon and myself to bring it to existence, but it was something special, something worthwhile, something I was just a little bit proud of. It wasn't my normal work, but it was something I rather liked.

Simon had liked it too, but I'd convinced him his gifts for his crush were more than enough. It would also be completely tasteless if we gave the girls the same thing. Not that I'd not done it in my previous life, but I'd been found out, and it had not ended with any happy women. Unhappy women could make your life unreasonably difficult if they wanted to, so we were doing what we could.

A waiter came by, looking me over, along with my gift.

"May I get you anything, sir?" he inquired, though he should have known the answer.

"No, not until my company arrives," I answered.

This particular restaurant was well outside of the city proper, on a lovely little hill overlooking it. The view was marvelous; however, the staff was less than impressive. I'd come here on a recommendation from one of my classmates, who had said that it was one of the best spots he knew of, and perhaps it was. Other than the stunning vista of Exion, the décor was nice, scents drifted toward me from the kitchen, making my mouth water ever so slightly, and it was a calm, relaxed atmosphere.

There was also the not-so-small detail that it was outside of city limits, one of the running requests from my professors of something I shouldn't do. Honestly, I didn't want to jinx it, but I was hoping we wouldn't have too many problems today. After all, I was here to meet a girl, not start a fight, burn something to the ground, or meet a monster of some sort. I would have to admit, though, that some of my classmates at times thought of girls as monsters.

Luckily, at least, I didn't have to wait too long for my companion to join me.

"Percival, it's been too long," Rowena said as she took her seat across from me, her chaperone looking on keenly from the side.

I didn't love the habit, but in some cases such people would be employed, particularly when, like us, two young people were officially courting and in public. During our dinner with the duke, such a thing hadn't been needed, since his people were there, or the carriage driver otherwise, but here one was deemed appropriate.

"You as well, Rowena. I do hope everything is going well?"

"Oh, quite busy, and everyone at the school is in a whole state. There's been some kind of change in the administration. People are saying the king himself is involved. Probably rumors, but you know how things are. How are things at your academy?"

"Well," I said. "I've actually been spending some time with people other than your brother of late. One of them even helped me to make this." With a light gesture, I offered her the small box.

"Lovely," she said, pulling open the lid with a small smile and admiring the runes on the inside. "What's it do?"

"Nothing much; just keeps itself clean and has a small lighting charm."

As she opened it fully, the latter came into play, a soft white light spilling over her features. The inner lid held a mirror, made to stay perpetually clean magically. Well, actually, I'd cleaned it manually, and it projected a tiny, almost infinitesimally thin shield over itself, repelling dirt and grime, but the effect was the same.

"So many little compartments," she giggled.

"I had to consult similar items, though I was told they were the right sizes," I admitted.

That too was true. It was made for jewelry, cosmetics, and all the little things women used to keep themselves looking nice. Personally, I thought it was all a bit much, particularly for a girl of her age, but it was the style. What did I know? I was a man in both of my lives and had no experience with that kind of thing.

"Thank you so much. I know just the place for it. Actually, there was something else I was hoping you could talk to me about though."

I raised an eyebrow. "What's that?"

"Do you know why I'm in town?" she asked.

"Not entirely, but I've heard a bit. Your school is taking a hiatus," I confirmed. It was part of the reason I'd asked her to meet me once I'd learned she'd be around.

I actually knew quite a bit. Her school had been really tied up with the now dead archmage. That death was a country-shaking event, still being kept under a shroud. People knew, a good number of people, but how exactly it had happened, who'd done it, and the like were still deeply secret. She'd even alluded to it earlier, to keep details from the public eye. They were getting out of school much earlier than normal this year.

"Well, Mother and Father don't have a teleport point near our summer home, so I'm staying in the city for now. They're trying to find me a tutor, but for rather obvious reasons, those are in very high demand right now."

"Yes, I can see how they would be."

"My brother will be around a bit as well, but he's not of . . . a very intellectual persuasion either."

"Indeed," I snickered. Lucas was a dyed-in-the-wool meathead; not stupid, but uninterested in things other than fighting.

"Would, would you be willing to help me with some of my studies . . . I mean, not the magic, but some of the other things. I really don't want to fall behind on math, civics, or the like. Sadly, I feel that many of my classmates will be doing just that too. Also, if you can make this," she said, pointing to the box, "maybe you can help me with my magical items? I'm always ever so behind in that class."

"Certainly," I said. "We can meet whenever we're able, and it always brings a smile to my face when you send me a letter. I may not know all that much more than you, but I'll help however I can."

I'd spoken before I thought too deeply about it, and found that I'd agreed to a perpetual study date. It would mean taking at least part of my days off whenever I had one for the rest of the year, at least if we followed the plan she was now laying out before me. Rowena had come prepared, with a small notebook full of days, times, and subjects, organized to a T. Well, at least it would keep me out of too much trouble with the school.

The waiter eventually interrupted us, and we gave him our orders. I had a pasta dish, served in a cream sauce with several herbs I couldn't identify. Rowena went with a type of fish, ever popular on the island, with a reddish sauce spread over it. After her deluge of plans, we moved to more background topics, the kinds of things one normally did on a date—fun anecdotes, recent events, even the news. By the time I left, I'd almost forgotten about the new thing I'd added to my schedule.

CHAPTER 8

★

DAYS OF PEACE

"I like your sister, but she's running me so hard I'm exhausted," I said to Lucas as I tossed the ball we were throwing around to him. Simon guffawed from the far side.

"I'm going to pretend I didn't hear that," Lucas deadpanned.

"I'm not," Simon said as he caught the projectile that had been aimed at his head.

"Don't tell me you're thinking of reneging on your agreement to help her with her studies?" Lucas asked with a slight glare as I caught the ball from Simon.

"No, but could you please ask her to put all her questions in one letter a day? I don't mind getting mail, but I'm just unsure how to arrange it all."

Letters were popular, unbelievably so, and there were several delivery times per day in cities. In our case, we were close enough to the city that we too were delivered several bags per day. I had mail at lunch, at dinner, and oftentimes in the morning with things Rowena had sent the night before. It would be obvious if I wasn't responding as I got them, but I was having to write enough letters a day as it was, and it was nonstop.

This was on top of the previous day's outing, where I'd gone to study with Rowena in person. She'd had a whole list of things, some of which I could do easily enough, but some of them were rather complicated. Her maids also spent a fair amount of the day shooting daggers at me because she'd gotten so close to me at the table, she was practically in my lap.

"I won't," Lucas said. "You'll just need to accommodate her. She's always been like that and always will, Percival. Do you know how many letters she sends me a day?" Lucas asked.

"More than three?"

"At least five. I shudder to think the savings our family would have in paper alone if she'd limit herself, but it makes her happy. You do want to make her happy, don't you?" That was a trick question if ever there was one.

"Of course—"

"Good, then you know what to do," Lucas said, cutting me off.

I wanted to sigh, but I'd really dug myself in deep enough already. He was my friend, one of the best I'd had in either of my lives, and his sister? Honestly, I didn't know quite what to think of Rowena. She was a nice enough girl, but too interested in me, not something I wanted now, or perhaps ever.

"Fine then, if that's what she wants, don't say anything. I'll just deal with the deluge."

"Good man," he said, laughing.

"Is more or less better?" Simon asked. "Honestly, my girl only sends me one or two letters a week. Not sure what to think of that."

"You'll have to answer that yourself," I said. "Personally, I think all girls are different, or they're really the same and just messing with us in some sort of conspiracy. It wouldn't surprise me in the least if I found out that older women told their daughters to be completely unpredictable, just to mess with us." That got me another round of laughter.

Like most good times, days passed like water through the fingers. Life was like that sometimes, always passing you by when you were enjoying it, always slowing to a stop when you were in pain. Before I knew it, another month had gone by and left me in its wake, looking about in confusion.

I sat on the afternoon of one of my days off, deep in my workshop at home. I'd already had today's study session with Rowena, and while she was clingy, I had to admit I enjoyed helping her. There was much for me to learn, things that were covered in her schoolbooks that mine didn't really touch on, particularly when it came to the specifics of magic and its limitations.

There was so much nuance when it came to the programming language that was the runic script. I simply didn't understand most of it, but I saw enough to know that nobody was using it to its full potential. I also got the distinct feeling that there were people in the world hoarding the best snippets of code like they were precious gold, which of course they were.

For example, I'd recently written a rather detailed code that made electricity, of all things. This was something nobody in this world used, and for good reason. There were so many better ways to light your home—and so much easier if you were rich, much safer too—that it had never caught on. Sure, some people knew that electricity existed, and some even knew that it could be used for some rather interesting things, but it was relegated to a curiosity in this world.

My purpose, though, would use it, for I was making a barrel. There were other, more effective ways to rifle a barrel than the setup I had going, but I didn't have those tools. They were expensive, and I wasn't exactly making a lot of these. For now, I was using a trick with knowledge gained by one Mr. Jstark (may he rest in peace) to get the rifling correct. Technically, it was called electrochemical machining, and it worked well enough.

I was also having to redesign the handle for my current project, the only one of its kind I could properly dig from my memory no matter how hard I tried. I'd seen too many diagrams, too many videos of how it worked, and it was ingrained there in my weird elvish brain. That said, I was really looking forward to when this project was done.

While that did its thing, I moved toward a project I felt would never finish. Ignus and the duke had finally come through with my propellants, and now it was time for ammo. How I missed the days when I could go to the store for this kind of thing. Then again, maybe not. Prices had been absolutely insane. Even if I had to do it all myself, having things delivered to me was . . . something.

"Um, it's getting late, Lord Percival," I heard from the door. It was a quiet, almost shy voice.

It was Kaylee. Of course, it was always Kaylee. The staff had gotten the memo that I was far more tolerant of her than anyone else. I turned to look over at her and smiled.

"Certainly, and please don't feel the need to call me 'lord' when we're alone." I'd told her before, and I was sure I would again.

"Oh, I can't do that. What if the housekeeper heard me? It would be no end of trouble." She made a placating gesture, and I simply smiled.

I'd still not yet figured out what to do about her. Perhaps I could get my father to recognize her one day, and that would be the end of this farce. Then again, I could just wait. One day I would be the one with the power to say who was my kin. Today wasn't that day, though, so I could only smile, smile and give her a fraction of the kindness she deserved.

CHAPTER 9

✷

SEASON APPROACHES

I put the final one of many, many documents Mrs. Rider had provided to the side. Over the past months, the housekeeper had done a magnificent job, at least as far as I could tell. The books were in order, nobody was complaining about her behavior in any way that I cared about, and things were running smoothly.

"Well, I would have liked to have finished sooner, but it's nice to finally be done with this chore," I said to her and put the papers away.

"Oh, I'm sure if you continue, you'll be an expert soon enough. You're already paying more attention than most, my lord," she retorted with a small chortle.

I didn't really think I was but shrugged. If something was worth doing, it was worth doing it right. It had taken so long because I honestly didn't dedicate the amount of time I needed to it. Add to that the fact that we were still gaining expenses when I'd started, and I really didn't understand certain aspects of them, and it had been a learning experience.

Had that been what my mother intended? She hated the Season with a vengeance, and getting me to do this was one of her most important chores of the year, but it also served me. Learning what I had would help me to manage a house in the future if I needed to. Normally it was the women who ran household expenses and the like, but being capable was a good skill to have.

The gendered division of labor was still a thing in this world, though it was perhaps not as extreme as it had been in my previous one. Women, particularly those who had magic, could and did rise to very high places in society. However that wasn't as common as it was for men, with many women opting instead to stay and manage households, raise children, and generally work at home. Mother was like that, selling her mana at times, and certain magical services only available to those with that power, but generally remaining at home while my father worked.

Within the majority of the population, those who didn't wield the power of mana, the disparity was far higher. The sad truth of the matter was that pregnancy was debilitating, and without a way to change that, disparities arose. There was of course a form of birth control in this world, though I knew it required magic to keep going, and as such limited itself by that fact to those who had power or money to buy it.

"Ah, where was I? Oh yes, good work, and you're sure we're ready for this year?" I continued, realizing I'd been lost in my thoughts for a few moments.

"Absolutely, of course we'll be having less visitors overall, so that will make things far easier."

I nodded. Even if my parents weren't around, that didn't mean I was getting the annual party season off. No, I was still expected to go and attend to everything. Though, this year I would be accompanying my grandparents and would be at their homes for dinners more than my own.

"On that note, have you received word on when my grandparents will be arriving?" I inquired, having not gotten that letter yet.

"Indeed, three weeks from now. They're arriving the day you get off from school. Isn't that wonderful?"

There was a zero percent chance that was unintentional. My father's parents might live in the city, but knowing that my maternal grandmother would be showing up just in time for me to have no peace at all during vacation really was a wet towel atop my head. At least Grandpa was coming, and he was an absolute blast to be around.

"*Wonderful* is a word one could use," I admitted.

"Oh, don't pout," Mrs. Rider said, admonishing me. "It's unbecoming, and I do hear your grandfather is bringing quite a few things with him." That got my attention fully. "Just a rumor though," she teased.

"Come now, you must share after saying something like that," I pouted this time.

"I was told you could hear the general news, but even I wasn't given details."

"Would you share them if you were?" I questioned.

"Of course not, my lord. I may respect you, but your parents employ me."

I laughed at her candor. "True enough. I can't blame you for that sort of loyalty."

"I think your grandmother wishes to inspect the staff, though, so we'll have to get them into top shape."

"You will indeed," I agreed. "Grandma makes Mother look like a kind, gentle soul. Though I don't expect she'll find any problems. I certainly haven't."

"You say that, but I'm worried about the new footman, Lord Percival."

One of the boys was new, but he was fine. There were standards, and while he didn't blow them out of the water, he was certainly well within them. If Grandma had any real problem with him, I might need to address it, but that wasn't an issue. I did worry, however, about my favorite maid, but even if she was found wanting, she'd stay. I would see to that personally.

"Trust me, it will be fine. He's not exceptional, but he'll do well enough, and with my parents gone we won't have many visitors this year. You've an entire year more to get him ready for a real Season and the madness that follows it. Just make sure everyone is ready like you always do, and let me handle her if she finds something she doesn't like."

"Not quite sure that will work..."

I snorted. "You've all been under my direct supervision for most of this school year, and shall continue to be for the coming winter. I may be barely a man"—Mrs. Rider raised her eyebrow but said nothing; I was only fifteen—"but I'm enough of one to stick up for my people when they need it."

"Well, if you say something like that to her, I'm sure we'll all come out all right. I'll do my best to make sure you need not though."

After a bit of an early dinner I returned to my school. I didn't eat at the house all that often, but there was always food of some sort around. The food made by the staff at home was also leagues above that made for us students. I'd spent years giving feedback to Sinea and the others, so they all knew what I liked. She, too, was still with us but had gone from the young girl I'd met as a toddler to a proper woman now. She'd even married a few years back, easily able to have a family with the fact that we were there so infrequently.

I reflected on that, how much people had changed over the years, how much I had. I knew that with the few drops of elven blood I had I would age slower than most—perhaps not much slower, but slower. Mother still looked a couple decades younger than she actually was, and Grandpa, though I knew he would be considered quite ancient by human standards, had only a smattering of grey in his hair. How much more would I get to see? Would it be like my previous life, where I lost loved ones one by one, or worse because of it? Some of my family at least had a good chance to keep pace with me, but not all of them, and not necessarily forever.

Putting those thoughts aside for now, I got into the little carriage that would return me to the academy and my friends, knowing I should savor them while I had them.

CHAPTER 10

TESTS

Word by word, I worked, pen scratching, ripping into the paper before me. Beads of sweat rolled down my forehead, for I'd been at this for hours, and while I loved this sort of thing, it was mentally taxing. My hand was cramping, eyes bothered by the constant staring at papers. I thought I'd had it bad before, but this was pure torture.

All around, the other students were also crouched over their papers, eyes locked onto question after question and essay after essay. This world had unfortunately come up with the idea of final exams, chances for the teachers to figure out how much of their work students had actually absorbed, not just short-term-memorized into one test or another.

There were some upsides, though, for nobody had invented the hated bubble sheet yet, nor would they if I had any say in it. Who was I kidding though? At some point someone would get the bright idea of multiple choice questions, and from there, it was such an easy jump into horrors beyond human imagining, such as standardized tests and odious government oversight of all education to the point of ineffectiveness.

Hours passed by while I worked, and before I knew it I'd reached the final question. No more paper left, no more queries to answer, I briefly looked over my work. There wasn't anything I wanted to change. Sure, I knew the professor would disagree with a few of my answers, but they'd been well written out and argued well; I was sure. Our professors were also fairly good, grading less on what they thought we should think and more on how we reasoned and understood the material.

Satisfied, I put my pen down, capping the ink, which I'd had to reload several times, and waited. Many of my fellow classmates were still working, still scribbling away as they worked their way through the sheafs of parchment to finish these exams. I had managed to finish first.

"Can I just say that I miss the practicals?" Simon complained as we found a spot on the grounds to lay down and unwind. "Those were way easier."

"I'm going to disagree with you on all points," I griped. "I've still got one left too."

"Which one?" Simon inquired.

"Combat."

"Those were two days ago though?" he said.

"Headmaster Logan is doing mine personally. I'm to meet with him this afternoon."

"I'll tell the others; we shall mourn your loss, my friend," Simon said with mock solemnity.

"Ah, there you two are," Lucas said as he located and plopped down next to us. "Ready to celebrate the end to this madness?" Lucas said as he located and plopped down next to us.

"No, we're planning Percival's funeral," Simon replied. "Headmaster's doing his combat exam himself."

"Do you have a preference on what flowers I should put on your grave?" Lucas joked.

"I'm sure it won't be that bad..."

When the time came I headed into one of the practice rooms. With a chuckle I remembered that this was the same one he'd beaten my ass in on my first day. Did he plan it that way? Perhaps, or perhaps this was just the most convenient one to his office.

The headmaster and Sir Kendrick both entered soon after, the former clad in a full suit of armor, the latter looking amused. Behind them came a smallish woman I didn't recognize.

"I have been personally tasked with your progress, and we shall see how it has gone. Your instructors have given their reports, their opinions, but the time is now." With those words a chest was slid across the floor to me.

Inside the box I found armor and weapons, and not just what I would have expected. The protection was not unlike what we normally used in classes, but I could tell that this was far more enchanted than was normal. Beside it, rather than a choice of weapons, I was presented with a short sword and a revolver, along with a box of rounds.

"Guns are quite dangerous," I pointed out to my opponent, and I began putting the armor on. He'd be cross if I didn't get ready while voicing my concerns.

"I'm well aware, Percival, and pleased to see you've learned to bring your worries to your superiors. Those rounds are loaded quite a bit lighter than is normal. They shall still function but will be weaker. Similarly, our armor is significantly reinforced, as is the warding on the training area."

"It's been tested?" I inquired.

"Of course, first on dummies, then upon myself. I even arranged for a priest, just in case something should go wrong."

I didn't know if I should be reassured or worried. A healer on hand meant that there was no reason for him to hold back, but it also meant that I couldn't hold back. If something went wrong, it could go very, very wrong, and this seemed foolish to me.

"This still seems foolhardy," I pointed out as I fastened the straps.

"If it bothers you so, you may leave the firearm aside," he finally said, and I did appreciate that he was listening.

"I shall."

"Very well. In that case you will need to demonstrate your proficiency later."

I heard a chortle from the knight who was standing off to the side and a sigh from the priestess as I picked up the practice sword.

"That sounds agreeable."

Leaving the other weapon in the box, we took our places on the practice mat. It might have been reasonable to think he would take it easier on me since I was deliberately denying myself one of my weapons, but I knew better. If anything, the headmaster would only push harder, testing the very limits of what I could do.

At a motion from the observing knight, we launched at each other. I would like to say that I won, that I'd grown enough to defeat the man who'd once trounced me so, but that would be a lie. At the first crossing of our blades it was clear he was still the superior here, the strike sending a wave up my arm. With a quick twist I brought the point of my weapon close to his chest, only for it to be parried with contemptuous ease.

We fought again and again—parry, block, attack, counterattack—on and on. The practice weapons flashed as we struck. I landed a few blows upon Headmaster Logan—quick moves into his guard where I could just reach—but it was no war I could win.

I was better than I'd been, better than I'd ever been, but I was still a boy to him. My arms were shorter, so I had a lesser reach, my movements were slower, and I lacked the power my opponent held. It would be years before I was fully grown. That wasn't all though. Our headmaster was a master of his craft, with decades of experience that allowed him to exploit every weakness with no hesitation at all.

Standing before him my arms shook from the strain, sweat pouring down my head like a river. There were bruises beneath my armor, though I could tell he hadn't hit me as hard as he could have. In the end, this was a test, not a beating, so he knew when and where to push, and how hard. If I were less experienced, I wouldn't have been able to tell, but now I could.

"Enough, you pass," Logan finally declared, and I sank to the floor.

"Thank you, sir," I said as I looked at the ceiling, trying to catch my breath.

"Ma'am, see if you can get him back up and moving. I'd like to finish these tests today," the headmaster said to the priestess, his voice taking on a gentle tone I'd never heard before.

She obliged, healing me, pumping me full of water and pickle juice (something I hated) and allowed the men to march me out to the shooting range. Of course our school had one of those as well, for guns were becoming ever more popular. Even if few knights used them, we were still expected to be familiar with them.

I did far better with the pistol than I had in the ring, nailing target after target. Some were thrown with a speed that would make pitchers on Earth weep in envy, and some were stationary, but they broke one by one. A few did escape me—shots not led enough, angles I didn't expect—but I struck well over ninety percent of the various targets.

And then it was over. I'd passed. As the others left, Sir Kendrick came to my side.

"You know, if you had actually shot at him, it would have been a failure on your part," he said.

"It would have been stupid, and needless," I pointed out. "We don't use bombs at each other either."

"That's why it would have been a failure, and you would have had to receive additional training."

"Glad I didn't fail then. I'm quite busy enough."

He laughed and patted my back. "We're always too busy. At least I can report to his Majesty that your training is proceeding well. Enjoy your break, Percival."

The healing did wonders, and while I was still tired that evening, I was released to go home. Some of the students would stay for a day or two yet, for official graduations, or for just the time it took for them to have arrangements made, but I had a place in the city, so I could leave promptly. Giving my goodbyes to my friends, and promises to meet up over the intervening Season, I got in a hired carriage and began my way back home.

About halfway there the vehicle slowed to a stop, and I felt something wash over me. A wave of drowsiness alarmed me, so I grabbed the weapons I had on hand. Seldom did I now travel without both my cane and my pistol, and drawing them both, I flew from the door, smashing it to bits as I prepared for violence.

"Peace," a voice called out from the roadside, some hundred or so feet ahead. It was one I recognized. "I did not come here to fight you, but rather to talk."

CHAPTER 11

MEETING ON THE ROAD

I pointed my weapons as the goblin slowly emerged from the brush. Behind me the horses and the driver slept, clearly knocked out by some spell.

"I didn't come here to fight," she said, hands open to show she had no weapon, as if she needed one.

"I've heard that one before," I replied.

"Fair, but if you kill me, my siblings will destroy your home. They know I'm here, and they know where you live."

I felt a twitch at that. The house was defended to an extent, yes, but it was no fortress. If they went there now, it was likely people would die. It was likely Kaylee would die. Did they know about her? I doubted it, but I couldn't risk it.

"And your *father* won't do so anyway?" I asked.

"He's not involved in this," she answered. She must have seen my brow raise at that. "I have several concerns, and . . . his temper got the better of him before."

"You mean he's a maniac, killing people when they displease him and with no concern for the lives of others."

"I still believe he wants a better world . . . I have to."

"What I believe is that that is what he's saying, what he puts out there to justify his actions. Perhaps on some level he thinks helping people makes it all right, has convinced himself, but that's not what he's doing. He's kidnapping humans, and I can guess what happens to them based on how many have returned."

This girl, goblin or not, bit her lip, clearly seeing where I was coming from. Good, very good. She had a conscience, and that was important, critical even. We didn't need to genocide their whole race, and I didn't want to. If we could just stop this "father" from his experiments, then we could find a place for them. It wouldn't be easy, but I had some pull, and if some of them joined us, it would be all the easier.

"Do you hate me for that? For allowing it to go on?" she asked, almost childlike, and she *was* a child in some ways, wasn't she?

I remembered him coming here, his initial escape. This girl was likely years younger than me. I might well be talking to a girl no more than ten years old, and even if they matured quickly, there could be some mercy there. If we could just bring them around to seeing that what they were doing was wrong, we could make those changes.

"Were you involved in the killing?"

"No, I couldn't stomach it. My duty is to protect our home." Excellent, she'd be the perfect one to turn.

"Then understand that what he's doing is dangerous. My people will continue to act, and if they find you have an army, you can't hope to defeat what will come for you. There can be another choice though; you can change things. We can find a place where your people can live in peace, without the fighting, without the hate. From what I understand you came from an island nobody else wants. You could return there, smarter than you were, and make it into something great without any more of this."

"I will consider that," she replied. "What I came to ask about was the strange ones you sent into the undercity." A start, but one I could work with.

"Strange ones?" I asked.

"They're not completely human, like us? They're different, and it looks like they did something to their ears. They've been killing our people so effectively, so how can you call for peace when you do something like that?"

"I don't know anything about that, unfortunately, but there are people I can ask. Don't expect them to stop though, not after the problems your people are causing." Also, ears? Not completely human? Was she talking about . . . "These strange people in the undercity . . . What else makes them different?"

"Father caught one, said he'd live much longer than was normal."

Oh, shit. "Elves? I promise you, I will bring that up to somebody. The fight, the one your sister was at—one of them was there. If they are who I think they are, they're our enemy too."

It didn't make sense. What was their angle here? I knew they'd been after the archmage, but now the goblins too? Were they just hunting potent mages? If so, that was a huge problem. Others would need to be warned because that would be the lead-up to a war.

"Very well," she said. "I don't suppose you'll agree to meet later?" she asked.

"The last time I went to a meeting with your people it didn't go so well."

"True. Will you at least let me leave peacefully this time?"

"You came in peace, you can leave in peace. Do think about what I said though; know that you have choices," I added. It wasn't like I had the backup to win for sure anyway, so a fight might well end poorly for me.

"I will." With those words she slipped into the brush, disappearing again.

I breathed deeply for a few minutes, stretching out my senses to their limits to look for any others, anyone who might ambush us. As I did, I heard the driver stir behind me.

"Oh, Lord Percival, what? Why are you out here, and why are we stopped? Did something happen?" he asked in quick succession, clearly understanding that something was off.

"It did, and we should leave with haste," I replied.

"Yes, sir, at once!" He snapped the reins, causing the snoozing horses to shake awake quickly as well. They seemed less bothered by the fact that they'd fallen asleep in the middle of the road.

As I walked back to the door of the carriage, I stopped to change his instructions.

"We've a new destination though. Take me to this address." I quickly jotted down where Ignus had his public offices—where the law enforcement was for the whole city—and he instantly recognized it as such.

"Yes, sir," he answered, and we began moving once more.

Now all I needed to do was figure out how I was going to explain all of this without causing another panic. I also needed to get Ignus and his superiors to agree to spare any goblins who surrendered. If I could do that, I could continue to try and get them to switch to our side in good conscience. I'd have to anyway, but I couldn't be sure how well I could feign loyalty to people I was about to betray.

CHAPTER 12

★

COMING HOME

Ignus seemed less than enthused when I shared with him my interaction. It was nice that he'd at least made a hole in his busy schedule for me, but that was expected. After all, it wasn't like I spent a lot of time bothering him, and never did we meet for some needless thing. Once his people had relayed who was there to see him, he'd quickly made the time and seemed satisfied that he had.

"It was good of you to try and convince them to surrender."

"I'm assuming it would be accepted then?" I asked.

"There would be some concerns, and I'd need to speak with his Grace for any formal arrangements, but yes, it is always better to turn enemies into allies rather than fight them." I sighed in relief at his words. "Of course, I would have preferred if you'd come to us first to confirm that before making offers . . ."

"Honestly, I wasn't sure I'd have many more chances to do so. It's not like I can just go down and find them with ease."

"No, honestly not, and our people have failed outright. Elves coming after them concerns me most though. Why would they do that? Why change their target? It makes no sense unless there's some other connection."

"What if there is?" I asked.

"Like what? It's not like Archmage Penumbra and this *father* have anything in common."

They did, though, and so did I. Both of them were old, powerful, and from Earth. How had the elves known that? And if they did, why not come after me? I was certainly a much softer target than either a hundreds-of-years-old archmage or an insane goblin magus and his army of mutant children. Heck, even with my family around and the guards, the attacks I'd seen against the former would have left me stone dead.

"Their mana," I answered. "It's the same."

Ignus popped his head up, staring at me.

"I'll admit I can't see it, but you shouldn't be able to either?" he questioned.

"I can't, but Archmage Penumbra confirmed it for me, and it's how Father and his people found me." At his raised eyebrow I continued. "Mine is also the same."

"Shit," he breathed, grabbing some files from his desk. "I'm not sure why it matters, but it could. You do have a knack for making friends, too, don't you lad?"

"A skill I've long cultivated," I assured him.

This conclusion raised so many questions though. How much did the elves know about people from Earth? Were they making the connection between us and the jumps in technology? If they were, it might be understandable that they were a bit antagonistic. Elves were longer-lived, but slower-growing. With humans gaining power, we could pose an existential threat, and the quick reproduction of goblins, according to stories, could be much the same.

The elven nations had their own hero, though, one who was almost certainly another reincarnator. He was supposed to be dead, but what if . . . What if they'd gained another, or their old leader had left instructions or something? Anyone coming from our world to this one would certainly know the danger, and he could have either been insane, like Parkov, or just misunderstood after so long.

"The look in your eye tells me you perhaps know something you're not sharing," Ignus said, pulling me from my thoughts.

"Nothing concrete, just suspicions is all."

He gazed at me like he didn't believe that for a minute. "If you know something, you need to tell me."

"Nothing I can put into words, but I think there may be a connection between our mana and something else. We're all . . . strange, the kind of people who make waves. What if there were others in the past like us, others who, for some unknown reason, caused them to react like this?"

"That seems improbable," he grumbled.

I just shrugged. "There's nothing else I can do for now, unless you have something?"

"No, just be careful."

I sighed in relief that he wasn't prying too much more and left. Between this meeting and my previous one, it was now getting quite late. Crossing the city this way and that wasn't instant, with the traffic from all the people arriving for the Season. Dozens of noble families, wealthy individuals who wanted to emulate them, and a veritable army of servants were all coming into the city. It caused an absolute disaster of congestion for a week or two as things began to get prepared.

It was nearly dark as we pulled into the house's drive, and I rubbed my head in exhaustion. Even if I'd done fairly little today, it was quite a bit of effort. Our cook, Sinea, would have prepped such a nice lunch too—all of my favorites. I'd have to apologize to her for missing that special meal. Something pleasant before my grandparents got here this evening.

That thought hit me as the driver opened the door. My mind spun. Perhaps I could avoid their attentions if they weren't here yet. A quick look showed that there were no other carriages present in the drive.

"Something wrong, my lord?" the driver asked.

"Perhaps not just yet," I said, hurriedly hopping down.

"Ah, very good sir. Would you like anything else?"

"No, no, go take care of the horses. I'm sure they're tired."

He chuckled. "Right you are, sir."

I hurried to the door. There wasn't a moment to waste. I needed to get ready, to tell the staff to prepare. Grandpa would be here any moment. He wouldn't be a problem at all, but Grandma had rules like a chef had knives—many and sharp—and we couldn't disappoint her.

Passing the empty entry, I hurried toward the central rooms. There would surely be someone here, and if there wasn't, Mrs. Rider's office was closest to the drawing room. As I entered said drawing room, I found them there. Grandma was about halfway through a sip of tea as I rushed through the door. She slowly finished the drink she was taking, eyes narrowed over the cup. As she put it down, I could see how her lips were thinned into a single line, displeasure written on her face. Beside her Grandpa seemed moderately tired, but also a bit amused. He loved antics in a way I never did, though I surely ended up in more trouble than he did.

"Good evening, Percival," Grandma said. "You're late."

"Ah, Grandma. Yes, I got a bit delayed with some meetings. I was unaware you'd arrived yet; I didn't see your carriage at all."

"A happy accident. Our boat made better time than expected, and we got here around noon. Hoping to see you, we came right over."

They'd been here for hours and hours . . . "Oh, I see. My apologies for not being here to meet you."

"Nothing else to say?" she asked.

I thought for a second. "Not as such, no." I then turned to my grandpa. "Grandpa, do you happen to have any books on elven history?"

Grandpa guffawed while his wife began to develop a twitch in her eye. You'd think after years of this they'd be used to me.

CHAPTER 13

✶

STRESSED

"You could have at least been here on time," Grandma complained, interrupting my attempt to change the subject.

"You were early. That is hardly my doing. I also would have liked to have been here to meet you, but as I said, I had a number of unexpected meetings. Not ones I particularly enjoyed either."

"Your teachers?" she asked.

"No, everything at the school is . . . well busy, but fine. I did quite well on my exams."

"Then why the questioning about history, Percival, my boy?" Grandpa asked, putting a hand on his wife's arm to forestall any further questions.

"Personal interest. I've been running into a number of things I think are somehow related to the old king," I explained.

"Oh, I see. That's not altogether surprising, as his inventions are famously important in society. He made the core after all, and so much else. Personally, I think it's all a bit exaggerated, attributing to one ruler everything his lands came up with or something like that, but I do have a few." Then he laughed. "Though you'll need to be able to read one of the elven dialects to understand them at all."

"I don't suppose you could teach me?" I asked hopefully.

"I could teach you to read pretty quickly, but the language itself is a complex thing, Percival, and I'm no expert."

"Certainly your school teaches it, though, and it isn't bad for a young man to learn another language. You'd be good to sign up for those," Grandma pointed out.

I briefly felt dizzy as I pondered the idea of adding more to my workload. Small sounds, like voices screaming "NO!" rang in my ears. Visions of my class schedule from the previous two years appeared before me, every time slot full, a few extra lines added on here or there for even more education.

"Oh, I'm quite booked already, Grandma, though they do offer it as an elective."

She looked at Grandpa and sighed. "Could we get some privacy, my dear?"

"Certainly," he said, and with a smile he wove a spell around us. That sort of thing wasn't odd, and most families had that spell on tap for when they didn't want servants overhearing what they had to say.

She patted the couch beside her. "Come here, Percival."

Hesitantly, I joined her, taking a seat as the haze pulled around us. As I did, she looked into my eyes, taking my chin in one hand and giving me a good once-over. She looked, really looked, before pulling me close and against her side.

"Grandma?" I said, almost confused.

"You look tired, son, so tired; tell me what's wrong." Her voice had changed from the harsh demands to something kinder, more gentle, something I rarely heard.

"What?" I asked, surprised.

"You must think me so unkind, don't you? How harsh I've always been, always demanding, but I've never tried to give you more than I thought you could handle—a push, but never one past what I thought you could take. Just now, though, you looked so broken. So, tell me, what is happening?" I tried to get over the whiplash as she held me close, petting my head.

"There's no time for anything," I answered. "Everything is falling apart, and there's no time for anything at all. Months going as fast as I could, and it still feels as if I've hardly moved."

"What in the world has you so rushed?" she asked.

So I told her. I spoke of the goblins, how I feared that soon they would come to the surface. I spoke of the former archmage, her death, the battle that had happened that day, the demand that I be properly trained. Even the elves that seemed to be attacking the city for some reason.

It would appear that they'd been unapprised of all the details, because I could feel the stress radiating off of them both. Most of this was secret, of course, but at the moment I wasn't sure I cared, and I trusted them both. Sure, Grandma was harsh, and Grandpa was a bit silly now and then, but both were good people, trustworthy. Neither interrupted with questions as I went on and on, letting loose all that I'd been worried about for what seemed like years now.

"They shouldn't be leaving this all on your shoulders," she finally said when I was done.

"There's nobody else who can do all of it. I'm the one who designed the weapons, who the goblins are so interested in, who the archmage left to be trained. There are others working, surely so, but they're only seeing part of it; we're all only seeing part of it. That can't last though. Factions like this won't stay still forever, and if we're not ready when it all comes to a head . . ."

"Who knows what would happen, but no, you're too young. Youths should get the chance at youth, not be forced into adulthood like this."

I laughed, for I'd been an adult already once, and I understood that well. Still, though, this body wasn't there yet. I was still growing, hormones still raging. Perhaps I needed to be as I was, but I wasn't there yet. Hopefully how I was would be enough, but I couldn't tell for sure.

"Well, there's only one thing for this," Grandma finally declared. "You'll be having nothing to do with this nonsense through the Season."

"Not sure I'll have much of a choice, Grandma," I complained.

"Perhaps, but you're not worrying about this nonsense more than is absolutely necessary. We'll be here, and it sounds like your paternal grandfather has already arranged some guards. We'll have to talk to him about that. You can also be sure I'll be talking to your parents about leaving you alone in your time of need—dammed irresponsible."

That brought a smile to my face, and even caused me to laugh.

"I did the finances for the house this year; rather fun in the end."

"I'll be having a conversation with your mother about that too," Grandma assured me with just a hint of venom in her voice.

"Tell you what, though, Percival, I do have something that might help you relax," Grandpa added. "I brought your project."

"Does it work?" I asked, not having had a chance to see the full-sized plane he'd ordered well over a year ago.

"Haven't had the chance to try it out yet, and I'd never do it without you anyway. Did find a place to set it all up though . . . Soon as you're ready."

"I'm ready now!" I said standing.

Grandma pulled me back onto the couch. "The only thing you'd better be ready for right now is dinner, Percival. You also can't test some fool flying machine that's likely to fall straight to the ground at night." She sighed, knowing how I could be when it came to fun things.

"She's right, my boy, but your excitement is right on."

"Rightly so," I agreed with my grandpa, eliciting a laugh from him and a sigh from Grandma.

CHAPTER 14

✶

A GOOD DAY

I awoke excited, for today was the day—the day I'd been waiting for, the day I'd spent years preparing. My clothes were laid out the day before, my whole schedule cleared, ready for the one thing I had to do today. After dressing I nearly skipped down the stairs, seeming to float, like I soon would fly, as I descended.

"You seem in a good mood this morning, sir," the maid bringing my breakfast observed, seeing the stupid smile plastered across my face.

"The best; today is the day!" I agreed.

"I'm glad to hear it. Will there be anything else?" she asked, quickly leaving as I indicated I was well.

The staff were always at arm's reach, close to us, but far. It was something I'd dealt with for years, and it still bothered me from time to time, but what was there to do about it? They had to maintain a professional distance, even if we were friends—almost—and in my case, sometimes, family. People I'd known since I first entered this world, who'd been there for my first steps, my first meals, all of the milestones of life, treated me as if we existed across a vast gulf. It was kind of sad.

Breakfast, on the other hand, was anything but. The first meal of the day was one of the most important in this world. While dinners and the like often held the spotlight, breakfast was still king. It was also the time of lovers, as many would meet to share their first meal, and the traditional time for dates. Some old notion about it being the right time to impress your loved one and make them think about you all day long. That notion was changing a bit here and there, but many still held to it. Arranging a breakfast was a serious affair, and sometimes a sign of an affair.

It was for that reason that the spread was so impressive—meats, fruits, nothing too heavy, nothing too complex to make, but all sorts of small dishes. I liked bread and had never found a proper way to make biscuits and gravy in this world—something for the to-do list. I took a few slices of bread and loaded them up with berries and a bit of honey before moving on to fish. Seafood was a staple in Exion, and probably every island city, but getting it light enough so it didn't weigh you down during the day was a skill mastered here. Some kind of citrus on lightly baked meat was just perfect for starting the day.

As soon as I could I gathered up my hat and cane and went for the front door, jumping the steps and landing at the bottom with a small push of my left foot. The carriage was only a few feet away, and the driver looked at me after the feat. While basically anyone with a physical enhancement-type magic could have leapt the seven or eight feet I had, it didn't mean they normally did. Wanton displays of power like that were a bit garish to a lot of sensibilities and mostly reserved for children or those entirely too worked up.

"Lord Percival?" he asked, looking at me, and he wasn't the only one, as a few people from the nearby street also stared.

"A fine day, isn't it?"

"Yes, sir," he answered awkwardly.

"You know our destination?"

"Indeed, Lord Percival. Please leave it to me."

Doing just that I sat behind him, letting the wheels clatter without any more input from myself. Grandpa had said it was all ready, all prepared for the moment of truth. All I needed to do was show up. We'd both put so much into this—money, time, expertise—all for the first flight of our creation. There was no way for me not to practically bounce in the carriage; well, more than carriages normally bounced.

Sadly, I wouldn't be claiming first flight in this world, since there were quite a few mages who'd flown before me. Nor would I be claiming first powered flight, as the elves would dispute that, claiming they had done it long ago, not that they still did. Regardless, I would still be making the first plane, to my knowledge, not some balloon.

As we pulled into the large field that would be our first testing ground, I didn't even let the driver stop before leaping from my cushioned prison. I could already see Grandpa there, by our project, talking to some man in a large leather overcoat.

"It's magnificent!" I enthused as I ran up to them like an arrow loosed from a bow.

"Slow down, boy! It's not going anywhere," Grandpa said, laughing as I skidded in near him. "And if your grandma sees you acting like that, she might well try to keep you from coming out again."

"I'd like to see her try. Wait, is she here?" I hadn't seen her, but I quickly looked around in mock panic. The only things around us were a few other carriages and a small storage barn. There weren't even any animals.

"Of course not," Grandpa said. "Do you think she'd want to go frolicking around a field at first light?"

"Only if she had no other choice." I turned to the other man and said, "My apologies, but I don't believe we've met; Percival." I extended a hand in greeting and with a smile.

"Pleasure, sir. Lionel Rightroad; I'm the test captain." As he spoke my smile faltered.

"Ah, so you'll be going after me?"

The two men exchanged a glance before my grandpa spoke to me again.

"Percival, this is an untested machine, and while I believe you'll do fine, and that it will work as we know it should, you simply can't be the first to use it. The danger may only be slight, but it is still dangerous."

"There is nobody who understands it better than me, with the only possible exception of yourself, Grandpa, and I'd dispute even that. You'll find that I'm also more than durable enough to survive any issues we might have today."

"Your grandfather has been training me on the controls for the last few weeks, even allowing me to use the undersized versions; and, while perhaps I don't feel confident understanding all the concepts as well as either of you distinguished gentlemen, I am quite durable myself."

"Is that so?" I asked.

"It is in—" There was a resounding *BOOM* as I punched him in the stomach. He looked down, having been blown back, but not out of his stance. "Kindly do not do that again."

"Percival," Grandpa said with clear displeasure.

"I am suitably impressed." I was also suitably infuriated. They were trying to steal this from me!

"Apologize."

"My apologies, Mr. Rightroad. I felt the need to make sure." The jerk was indeed tough enough to survive a crash, unfortunately.

"Let us put it behind us, shall we?" the man said magnanimously.

"Very well, is everything ready?" I asked them.

"Should be," Grandpa answered.

"You've already done the full check too?" I inquired, almost hurt. They were pushing me out of my own project, and he was supposed to wait for me.

"Well, not this morning, but when it came in last night—"

"Before every flight," I insisted. "Let's do it again, just to make sure."

My plan was a simple one, but one that I was going to do.

"He's not wrong, sir," Lionel said with a shrug. "We always do the same thing with ships."

"Fine, fine," Grandpa agreed with a huff.

They watched me like hawks as we walked over to the plane, the first plane in this world, and began to examine it. I was stunned, thrilled, for it was a thing of beauty. On the outside it looked like something from World War I, but inside it was filled with magic. Magic devices made up the motor. Pulling it rather than an internal combustion engine, making it near silent, they ran the controls, moving flaps, adjusting speed, all of it. Motorized versions would come, I was sure. Soon enough, but this one wasn't that.

We took our time going over every inch, with me pointing out small changes, things that were just a bit different from our models for one reason or another. The changes were few, but they were there, for no model really could do a perfect job. I even looked over the wheels, made from some rubber-like substance that I was told had come from a magical beast. Though I looked, I couldn't find any flaws of note. There were a few marks from shipping, places where it had been moved or put together, but all looked perfect.

In fact, I took so long going over every crease and crevice that they moved back a bit and began talking. Perhaps they were satisfied with it, but I wasn't, because I wasn't supposed to be the first. A horse whinnied loudly from where our carriages were parked, and grandfather looked up. Horses got into such states often, kicking each other or making noise, and it was the perfect time.

I hopped from the wing into the small cockpit, which had been made for two but only needed one, and hit the controls as fast as I could. Mr. Rightroad might have been tough, but I doubted he was as fast as me, and I was right. The power flipped on before he even realized what I was doing. The silent nature of the startup was key. There was no roar of an engine, no thudding of blades, no delay time. I just began to move. Grandpa barely had time to register the other man's movement before the plane was in full throttle, pulling me down the runway as fast as a speeding horse.

Lionel was shouting curses, Grandpa was yelling, and I was laughing manically. Today was a good day indeed.

CHAPTER 15

GROUNDED

Faster and faster I moved, the wind reaching a peak until I felt it. The sensation of the wheels leaving the ground was magnificent, the bumps changing with the wind as I began to climb, away from the dirt and into the sky. It wasn't fast, not like the insane speed jets from Earth, but just a few dozen feet.

"Percival, get back here this instant!" The sky roared as my grandpa stopped yelling and began to cast spells.

The field before me was massive; some kind of fallow farmland, hundreds of acres of it. Presumably, this was so we could do slow and steady testing, a smart thing, and build up to real flights. For me, it meant that I had plenty of room to keep going as long as I wanted, the open strip giving me ample room and wonderful views.

For a moment I considered taking off for real, climbing into the clouds, soaring with the birds for an hour or two. Then I came to my senses. That wasn't why I had done this. What I'd wanted was the first flight, the first time up, the proof of it, and I'd gotten that. If I kept pushing my luck, I might never again be allowed to fly. Well, I might not be allowed to anyway for a good while, but I'd accepted that.

With a sigh, I brought the plane down, slowly, with exceeding care. The wheels bounced a bit as I slowed, jostling me in the small pilot's seat. As quick as it had happened, it was over. Only mere moments of full flight time, but it was enough. I easily beat the twelve seconds the Wright brothers had managed, and that was good enough for me.

Once I was back down, I turned the plane around and began to coast my way back. Grandpa was going to be furious, but there was no reason to delay. Best to just take my lumps and be done with it. It took far longer to return than it had to flee, but I was aided by the fact that they'd chased me a good ways. As I pulled up I could see my grandpa fuming, teeth clenched together but no longer yelling.

"Of all the foolish, irresponsible, insane stunts to pull, Percival! I cannot believe your gall," he began as I got out of the seat and hopped down.

"I hope you understand why though," I replied calmly. "After so many years, I had to be the first, even if it was only for a few seconds."

"You could have been hurt; you could have died," he continued.

"That seemed improbable," I said. "We've tested this plane as much as we could have without actually testing it. It's also the reason I didn't go any higher than I did."

He looked particularly peeved when I didn't whine, complain, or try to weasel out of anything. "That isn't an excuse for your actions."

"No, it isn't. I'm merely explaining my thinking. I fully expected you to be furious and am willing to accept punishment," I told him with a shrug.

"You will not be flying again for the foreseeable future," he began, and I nodded. That was obvious. "I may tell your mother," he continued, which resulted in another nod from me. "Bah! Do you know how hard it is to punish you when you're like this?"

"I do," I said, chuckling, unable to contain my amusement.

"Not even sorry, are you lad?" asked Lionel, beginning to look over the plane.

"No."

"Perhaps we should tell people that Mr. Rightroad here was the first up. How would you feel about that?" Grandpa threatened.

"*I* will be telling nobody any such lie, and if they believe you, I will still know the truth."

"Your mother is going to tan your hide," he went on.

"Perhaps, but she won't be around for some time; she's skipping the Season, remember?"

Grandpa twitched, knowing I was right.

"I'm going to look this over, because so help me, if you've damaged it . . . You are to find somewhere by the barn to observe and remain there until I can figure out what to do with you."

It took a while, but in time he joined me as Mr. Rightroad got in and took off. This particular flight was much more by the book than mine had been, with the pilot having ample time to slowly go through the procedures we'd set up beforehand. Much like my first go, Lionel only went a few feet up at first, before returning to the ground. With each successive trip up he took, though, he climbed higher, and on trip three he was circling the large field at a few hundred feet.

I looked on with a smile. Even if I wasn't going back up today, I could still appreciate seeing my work—great work—and just the way it was intended. Nobody was doing anything fancy in the plane yet, but that didn't matter. The huge step we were taking was enough.

"Magnificent," Grandpa muttered.

"It is," I agreed.

"You could have been up there by this point. Still certain your acting out was worth it?"

"Every bit."

"You know we might forbid you from going up ever again after that nonsense."

I just laughed at that threat. "How long have you known me, Grandpa? If you try to keep me grounded for too long, I'll just make my own."

Only a couple years away from legal adulthood, that threat was just a bluff. I had the earning potential, the know-how, and the expertise from our work already to make a plane myself. It would take longer, and it probably would not be as good as what the two of us could do together, but it would fly. Of that I had no doubt.

My answer earned me a slap on the back of my head, but that was fine. Grandpa knew that I cared for him, and for the rest of our family. He also knew that I was stubborn as a mule and smart enough to get myself into trouble. We'd spent far too long around each other for him not to get that.

"You could at least try to apologize," he said in a gruff tone.

"I'm not sorry for what I did, Grandpa. To lie about that seems wrong to me. The lie would be worse to me than taking the plane up like I did. I am sorry for making you angry, though, and don't intend to repeat myself."

"Well, even if you never learned obedience, at least you learned morals," he groused.

To that I just answered with a small smile. He hadn't realized yet that he would probably be the one blamed for not driving obedience into my head. He wasn't. As someone who'd already lived a good part of another life, it was impossible for me to abide the kinds of restrictions people wanted to put on me, but Mother, and especially Grandma, would place the blame soundly at his feet.

CHAPTER 16

★

DESIRES OF LIFE

"It actually works, like properly?" the girl sitting across from me asked over the table.

"Indeed, we had a demonstration for some of the more technically minded men from the Royal Society just earlier today. Perhaps my project isn't impossible for them to have considered, but they're all quite surprised," I said. "You'd think that with all the papers my grandpa has published they would've expected this."

The girl's father, some lower-end noble, laughed from a couple seats down. "Ah, I might shed some light upon that. You see, people have been reading his papers, well a few of them, but they discounted that it actually worked. Normally, we see such things coming from well-known inventors, and while your grandfather may be well known for his interest, he isn't well known for his inventions." He looked at me more closely before continuing. "However, I have heard some of the most interesting rumors about you . . ."

"Perhaps I'm a bit clever, but I've not made that many things," I demurred, hoping to keep from getting too much attention.

My date for the evening took a moment to stop giving the girl who'd started talking to me the stink eye and chuckled at my remark.

Rowena had been happy enough to accompany me to this event but had been significantly less thrilled when she'd seen the seating arrangement. She was getting a bit on the possessive side tonight, and having me seated next to a girl who'd tried flirting the second we came in the door didn't sit well with her.

Not that I really blamed her. I suppose if I'd been out with her and someone had started making eyes at her, I'd have been rather cross myself, but it was behavior to note. The host for tonight was the Murkshire family, and it was clear that their daughter wanted something. Perhaps her family had put her up to it after hearing about the flight test she was now inquiring about; or, perhaps she had herself.

To be quite honest, I barely knew them, having seen said daughter, Lucy Murkshire, at a few events over the years but hardly ever talking to her. She had a brother a few years my senior who'd attended the same school as me, but I don't think I'd ever spoken to him either, just someone known in passing. Her uncle, though, was a common sight at Royal Society meetings, running in much the same circles as my grandpa.

"I don't suppose you'd be willing to show me this flying machine of yours?" Lucy asked, batting her eyelashes.

"You're welcome to come to any of the demonstrations we've planned. They're open to the public," I answered. Telling her flatly that I wasn't interested would be rude, but agreeing would create a whole slew of other problems; and honestly, I didn't know this girl at all.

Once more I thanked my experience from Earth for saving me. Most boys my age would see a moderately pretty girl making eyes at them and do something stupid, but that was a lesson I'd already learned from my first adolescence. Perhaps I'd never been the wisest or cleverest person, but I'd made it to adulthood, and if you did that, there were at least a few things you'd get clued in on.

Like the fact that this girl probably didn't care about me at all, not really. Planes were going to be big, and while a lot of people were writing them off, as they had on Earth, some weren't. Those who joined the flight industry early would soon find themselves at the head of new, huge investments. Cargo transport, private transport, military. The options were there, and I had the benefit of hindsight to know where to push.

Not everything would be the same—magic changed so much—but many things would be. Air travel, for example, would only be really good at medium range. For cross-continental or super long-range travel, magic gates were basically unbeatable. But, for something like my family's yearly trip to Exion? Shortened by days. Military applications would be huge, too, as few mages could fly, and exploiting the air would be a force multiplier like no other.

"Are you sure nothing else could be arranged?" Lucy pushed.

"Unfortunately not," I replied. "There are quite a lot of interested parties, and it's simply not feasible." I didn't add that I didn't want to. This girl was causing me problems, and I didn't want more.

Dinner after that was fairly bland. I'd made it clear to this family that I was unwilling to give them what they wanted, something I'd had to explain to others. Seeing that they could only make inroads through proper public channels, my hosts politely cut off their attempts.

"I'm sorry about that," I said to Rowena as we rode home. "Had I known they would use such tactics, I would've found a way to decline the invitation."

She looked across the carriage at me and chuckled, not her normal high-pitched laugh but something altogether less kind. "Oh no, seeing you deny them like that made the whole thing worthwhile. Did she really think that was going to work? Honestly, I feel a bit insulted on your behalf."

"On a lot of boys my age it would've worked," I informed her. "Boys tend to be rather foolish when it comes to girls."

"That's what I like about you," she told me, leaning in and kissing me so suddenly I didn't know what to make of it. One second she'd been leaning forward to talk, the next she was practically in my lap. "You're not like others."

"Rowena," I said, leaning back from her.

"Stop being such a prude. I know you're holding back, but I don't know why. I can tell you like girls, so it's not that."

I wanted to scream at her that I was far older than her, but that wouldn't make any sense. She wouldn't understand rebirth, and telling her now seemed too much of a danger to me.

"If you still feel this way once you're fully of age, we'll talk, but I don't want to lead you on." I'd always intended this to be mostly for show, something she had to know.

"Oh, now you are the silly boy," she said as she curled up in my lap, refusing to move. "You're not leading anything. I am. I'm the one who chose you, not the other way around." She turned a bit to poke me in the cheek playfully.

"And when exactly did you do that?" I inquired.

"Do you remember when we first met?"

"You asked me to beat up your brother, if I'm not mistaken," I answered.

"And you agreed perfectly. I had an inkling then, one you've only confirmed over the years. No reason to lie, but I've had crushes on other boys. They've all just come up . . . short. You, though, have always been what I wanted—mature but silly, kind but dangerous, cleverer than is good for you."

"I'm not sure that's entirely healthy . . ." I tried, hoping to get her to at least consider the situation.

"It is. It will give me exactly what I want out of life."

"And what is it that you want out of life?" I asked, blinking at her immediate response.

"A home, a good husband, a few children. That's about it, actually."

"That's . . ." I wanted to say "horribly stereotypical" but couldn't. ". . . not much."

"It is more than most people get, Percival. I mean, I'm sure I'll do other things, but that's the core of it. Mother managed it, and she seems quite pleased with life."

"You don't want to study magic, or invent, or—"

"I've an aunt who is like that; she seems rather unhappy. Not sure if that's because of what she does or because she's just a miserable old coot, but no. Honestly, I'm middling at magic at best, and like I said, I'll do other things. I'll still do magic, still try to improve myself, but I'm no genius, and no inventor. It seems better to me to instead bring what light I can to the world than to do things I don't want in an attempt to prove I'm someone I'm not."

"That is not the answer I expected," I admitted. "That you just want a husband and children."

"Not today, obviously, not for a couple of years."

"And what do you want today?" I asked, hoping for something slightly more understandable.

"The man courting me to wrap his arms around me properly, rather than keep them to his sides like he's afraid of me," she answered in a snarky tone.

With a snort I did so, relaxing them around her in a gentle hug.

"Good, we'll have you trained yet," she said as she curled up against me, laying her head upon my chest.

CHAPTER 17

★

SEWER SIGHTS

Greta slid through the sewers. She hated coming out here. It wasn't like the surface, where there was fresh air and the bright open sky, and it wasn't home either. Father at least kept the den well cleaned; some of the less intelligent of her kin might have made messes, but he made sure they cleaned them up. The sewers, though, were filled with filth.

As she moved, her glasses slid through various lenses, which were moved and flipped by a slight expenditure of her will. Each was special and suited the purpose for which it was made. She'd been using some lenses that enhanced her night vision, but now something more was needed. This time she needed her most amazing lens.

The crystal she'd acquired from a shop had been so interesting. How oddly it glowed. Even Father had liked it and had remarked on how it seemed to react not to light, but to heat. Whoever had put it in the shop had clearly not known just how it could be put to use, but she'd figured it out, and now it added to her arsenal.

"Quiet, slow," she told the three others who were following her; they were among the smarter of her burrow.

Unsurprisingly, her change in lens had shown her that one of the tunnels was hotter. There'd been a scent of something burning, but this confirmed it. Someone was fighting down here. Their fight had been close, close enough that the stones were still warmed by their passing, and close enough to follow. Brilliant spots in her vision spoke to flames licking the wall, possible to follow by smell perhaps, or the soot stains, but so much easier with her invention.

As one, the four goblins slinked down the tunnel, watching corners and chasing what was down here. The hunters—possibly human, possibly not—had been a problem, a real one. Local humans were bad at finding their foraging teams, but these hunters had chased them down, causing many deaths and more injuries. Even big brother Sigmund had taken a blow from them and had luckily survived to tell the tale.

"Greta, we need to hunt their hunters. As the cleverest of my children, find them, destroy them." That was what Father had said, and so she would.

Could he have done it himself? Certainly, and he had taken one of the teams out, but he had other things to do, important things. It was also good to let the young build themselves up, grow stronger to strengthen the burrow as a whole.

She put those thoughts to the side as the sounds of battle began to echo through the sewers—the whoosh of spells and the loud reports of guns resounding faintly at first, but growing rapidly in volume and intensity as they moved. Whoever was fighting was near, very near. Comparing a mental map of this part of the undercity with the signs of fighting, Greta had been led to a conclusion about where they'd gone.

The cadre of hunters were sidled up, lying on a lip that overlooked a drop into a huge holding and distribution tank that led to the battleground. She'd studied the build of it a couple years ago, a rather clever bit of architecture that served several purposes in making the whole city's wastewater system far more efficient.

"Capture, don't kill. We need to interrogate them!" one of the fighters said. He was a huge man in a dark uniform before he threw another fire spell.

It was four on ten. Unfortunately, the four all had power, while the ten had only two individuals with the blessing of magic. Normally, that powerful tool would be enough against even such odds, but there had been a change. The larger group had new weapons.

A trill ran up Greta's spine when she saw them, weapons just like that boy had had, beautiful mechanisms spitting fire and death. Father had been injured by one of these, but Greta had failed to get a proper look then. Oh, how she wanted a proper look. The massive increase in firepower was evening this playing field so well, and she wanted one.

While she looked on, several of the uniformed enemies fell to those she was hunting. The four had been reduced to two, bullets shredding a pair of their companions to ribbons. The leader kept shouting, kept commanding, until two became one, and finally the last fell to the ground, body broken and bleeding.

As the uniformed men tried to check for signs of life, finding one of their enemies still breathing and beginning to patch him up, something pressed the outside of Greta's leg. One of the three she'd brought with her, Gar, her favorite among the males in the nest, had pressed himself against her. That wasn't unusual. In such small confines contact was constant, but what wasn't was his position. His member was poking her leg, arm snaking near hers.

She let out a harsh but low hiss, warning him off. There was a time and place for flirting, and this wasn't it at all. Smarter than most of her kind, perhaps, but still a male, still enamored with lust. That was fine, good even, but so was stealth, which they needed presently. Out of the side of her vision, though, she watched him. He was studying her, watching where she was, seeing what she saw.

The uniformed men finished hauling the living and the dead quickly to another tunnel, one which led to the surface after a cursory search around the pit they'd been fighting in. Not that they could find anything in the muck. After giving them a minute to fully vacate, she looked at the males.

"Follow behind them, go quiet. I return to tell Father of this." It was best to keep her statements short and sweet just in case they were difficult for the others to understand. They all offered affirmatives, and she slipped away back to the nest.

"No, humans fight one another more than anything else," Father corrected her when she told him what had transpired. "Are more of the hunters around?"

"No sign of them, Father," she replied.

"Good girl," he said, patting her head. "Make sure the rest of the team has returned and your task is complete. He even patted her head when he spoke. I knew I could trust you."

She bounded to the opening of the nest to check, finding her sister on guard.

"They're back," Sasha told her from the front door with a horrid smile playing on her lips.

"Why are you smiling?" Greta asked her sister.

"Hehe, you'll see."

With a sigh, she left to wash and go rest. It had been a long day. There was even a little soap, stolen from somewhere or other. Father used it, so she used it, too, as did some of the others who were more clever. Too many ignored it, washing only with cold water from a small pipe.

Greta returned to her own personal space, a carved-out hollow near the center where Father lived. As a female and one of his favorites, she'd gotten a prime location. She wasn't surprised to find Gar standing there holding something. He, too, it seemed had washed with soap while she reported to Father.

"Gar," she said in a cold tone, his antics from earlier still clear in her mind.

"You wanted this, right? I bring it to you." He held out his hand, revealing one of the weapons, it, too, well cleaned. "One of the soldiers dropped it." His grammar was imperfect, but the gift was not. Gifts she got, more and more as she grew older. The males of the nest brought her food, or shiny things, or whatever they liked. They also liked to do as he had and get too close to her, or make big shows of their power, physical or otherwise, to get her attention. Frankly, it was a bit tiresome and stupid.

What none of them had ever done, though, was try to figure out what *she* wanted. They thought of themselves, brought her things *they* liked, but Gar had brought her something he thought she'd like; the difference was night and day. She loved her sister for how her sister thought about things, and now Gar was thinking, too, and thinking about her.

"It is beautiful," she said, taking it carefully from his hands before turning to her door. It was a curtain. She'd seen the humans doing it and liked the idea, so she used the same thing to separate her space from others.

She stopped as she crossed inside, looking back through the curtain. Gar stood there, looking a bit dejected that she'd taken the item and said little else. Before he turned to leave, though, she spoke again.

"Coming inside?" After all, the little gun wasn't the true gift he'd brought her. He'd given her consideration, something far more valuable than a trinket.

CHAPTER 18

✶

GRANDMOTHER'S DEMAND

"All right, Percival, the time has come to host an event," my grandma told me one afternoon. She was making an awful habit of interrupting my personal words on an almost daily basis.

"You're hosting something?" I asked.

"No, you are."

I was stunned, flabbergasted, and honestly a bit taken aback. "Grandma, I live alone, and I know absolutely nothing about hosting any such thing. Normally, isn't that something whole families do?"

"It is," she replied. "Normally your wife would handle most of the arrangements, but since you're still unmarried—"

"I'm not even of age yet—"

"Don't interrupt," she said, interrupting me. "Since you're unmarried you'll need to take care of the arrangements yourself. I'll be about, so you're welcome to come and ask me any questions you may have, but I'm expecting you to do most of it without any input on my part."

I had hoped, longed, for the Season, for the break from the unending schoolwork and people trying to shove more things into my brain, only for my dreams to be dashed upon my grandma's desires. I wasn't about to give up that easily, though, and if she insisted, well, I could certainly make something everyone would remember.

"Honestly, Grandma, I've no desire to do this at all," I complained.

"Of that fact I am acutely aware, but you still must. It's only one evening, Percival. You should manage without issue. You've a competent staff, a good cook, and I know for a fact that you've been to enough dinners and parties that you should have no questions at all about what to do."

"Really, shouldn't I be allowed a break from the work?" I pleaded.

"One never gets a proper rest, Percival, not ever. Though, if you truly desire one, make one. Make an event that you think is 'fun.' So long as it works with what others will expect, I'll have no complaints." At my raised eyebrows she continued. "Just make sure not to do anything inappropriate or extreme."

Well, that was something. Grandma was insisting I put on some event, but allowing me almost free reign here, something that I could consider enjoyable. Most people, in either this world or Earth, wouldn't have been terribly excited by my playing with machines, but perhaps we could, so something related? I needed something others would find enjoyable, too, since friends having fun around you almost always meant you'd have some fun as well.

"I need to think on this."

"Very well."

So that afternoon, think on it I did. I made my way down to my workshop, and as I considered planning a party, I brought out the project I'd been playing with for some time. Most of the internal mechanisms were done, but it needed ammunition, so as I began to shape those shells, I thought.

As my hands worked, my mind wandered, the rote exercise allowing me to drift on daydreams to an extent, only surfacing briefly to take a measurement or check diameters. Many years ago, before the current kingdom I knew, there had been decadent parties, but that seemed wrong. I didn't have the facilities or the funds to throw something completely boggling, which would take a lot of magic anyway. More recently, helping those weaker than you, or at least not showing off how strong you were, was considered more gentlemanly. Could I do something with that?

So what, a bake sale? The very thought of that made me snicker, and I ruined one of the casings I was making. No, that wouldn't work, but something charity-like certainly would. If people thought they were doing something for the poor, but didn't need to interact with them, that would be best. Even in this world, the rich liked to pretend the poor didn't exist, at least not somewhere they could interact.

Then it hit me, something quite obvious. I'd need to acquire a few things here and there—a proper venue, some interesting items . . . Pretty sure I could manage at least some of the latter easily enough. We'd also need drinks and snacks; though, not necessarily the full-blown meal that others would likely expect. Oh, and instructions for everyone. Yes, that could indeed be fun, and we would be doing something for others at the same time—the best kind of fun.

I could ask Simon to aid me with this, and pay him to make some items, or make them with him. The fact that they didn't come from stores would only add to the perfection of this idea. One or two others I could make myself; no problems there. In fact, it might be best if I leaned on the contacts I had at school or others my age for most of this. That would look good too.

By the time I emerged from my workshop to tell my grandma what I'd come up with, she'd left. After all, she had her own life to live and things to do. Mrs. Rider, however, found me looking about and stopped.

"Something wrong, sir?" she asked.

"No, not at all, just lost track of time."

"A surprisingly common thing to happen," she agreed with a smile.

"She left me with a task. I'd like to run some ideas by you and Sinea first. After dinner, perhaps, if that's all right. Never done something quite like this, and I find myself in need of advice."

"Of course, my lord. I'll be happy to help in any way I can." She looked on knowingly, and it wouldn't surprise me in the least if Grandma had told her about my assignment.

"I need to write some letters . . ." I muttered, and she bid me farewell.

First, I wrote one to my grandma, explaining everything in detail, all of my ideas. We were going to need to explain them to others, too, so trying with her first would be best. None of it would be too expensive—a rented ballroom or some such, some basic provisions, a handful of hired staff, all very manageable within cost for something like this. To this I added a list of questions, such as how and where to send things, her thoughts on if my plan would work at all.

Afterward, I began writing a few drafts to friends whom I'd need to participate. Simon was first, since his skills would be excellent, if not strictly needed. Then, my dear betrothed and her brother would receive a pair. On a lark, I began to form the guest list: the duke, seeing as I was on good terms with him, and Mr. Ignus, seeing as he would probably interrogate me about anything I sold, even if it wasn't dangerous or illegal; a few of my teachers might be interested as well; and though I feared to even try, I drafted a letter to Headmaster Logan, scared of the idea he might actually take me up on it.

With plans in motion, I sat back. Sure, there'd be a good bit of work to do, but most of it was easily manageable. At least I hoped it was. That's what we had help for though. Be they friends or family or just those working for us, to set us on the right path when we began to do something stupid.

CHAPTER 19

✯

MEETING PRISCILLA

"Hello there, my friend," Simon said cheerfully as I joined him at the small room in his home where we'd agreed to have our meeting. While his face smiled, his eyes held a hint of irritation.

"So, you're this Percival I've been hearing about. I heard you assisted my Simon with those lovely little flowers he gave me," a high voice added from a corner behind me.

I turned to see what could only be Priscilla, Simon's girlfriend. She was taller than I'd expected and lithe like a tree, long, but graceful as she moved across the room. Blonde strands of hair fell lightly over her shoulders, straight and silken. Her gown was simple but well made, not ostentatious, but enough to show she was someone important.

"Priscilla, then? Thank you for convincing Simon here for me." At my words the young man in question punched me in the shoulder.

"I would have helped anyway..." he griped as Priscilla approached us.

"Of course you would have," Priscilla said. "Helping orphans? I've seen enough of you to know that the few moments of your time this would take wouldn't have been enough to stop it." She leaned in to whisper to him. "But you'd have complained the whole time."

"Don't worry, Simon, I'll make it up to you somehow," I said, trying to placate my friend as he pouted.

"Oh, how?"

"Want a gun?" I asked. On Earth that suggestion would have sent people raving, but he was much like me and, honestly, probably had an arsenal of blades at his disposal.

"No, that's your thing, not mine. You had some models of those planes, though, right? Don't suppose you'd be willing to share a scaled-down one with me?"

"Easily done."

I could see the glimmer in his eyes, and his girlfriend shaking her head. He'd been trying to make a golem, something we weren't allowed to do, but one of my toy planes? That was perfectly allowable, and honestly, I owed him big for this, and for the gifts he'd helped me with for my lady friend.

"If you two are done, do you mind inspecting these?" Priscilla asked, motioning to the table.

I nodded and began to go down the line. Each of the small items he'd put magic into were of my own design and build, attempts at art. I'd based them off of pieces from Earth, some modern art swirls and twists, and some more like odd mathematical shapes people had come up with. Each was unique for this world, clearly something made for the joy of creation itself, but not fitting in clearly with any known aesthetic.

"They're weird," Simon said.

"Just fun shapes," I said. "I think they'll do all right."

"Any magical item sells well," Priscilla pointed out. "And I've talked to some of the other priests. We won't be buying them, but we're making sure to encourage those who might. The fact that these are pretty simple tools won't hurt either; they're something anyone can use."

"Anyone with magic," I pointed out.

"Anyone rich enough to be at your little party. Those who don't have magic can just hire mages to fill them," she said with a shrug.

She wasn't wrong either. Most of the wealthy were magical, and if they weren't originally, they ended up so in a few generations by interbreeding with magical families. Magic was power, pure and simple, and there was nothing that would promise your family long-term success more than having that power.

On the outside it might have seemed that our country was a monarchy, and to an extent that was true. More importantly, though, it was a magocracy, the power of mana infusing all of those who held important offices. Here and there non-magical folk, skilled workers or intelligent folk, would slip into power, but they didn't hold it. No, they were one-offs, the exception to prove the rule. It was families like mine that held sway over governance in the end.

"Well, it is as you say," I agreed after thinking it over.

"Of course, but do you mind if I ask a question about all of this?" Priscilla inquired.

"Go ahead."

"Why are you doing this?"

"Priscilla," Simon said tiredly, "you're being rude."

"I mean no insult. Actually, I think this is just the sort of thing we should do more often, but why?" she pressed.

"My grandma insisted I host an event, some kind of coming-of-age thing, so I'm doing it my way, not hers. Sure, it will be odd to everyone, but it'll be fun, and we get to raise funds for a good cause."

"Yes, I'm sure the Shield will be happy with the additional funding for their orphanage. Though I hope you're not thinking of pulling money off the top?" she asked, looking me over suspiciously.

Charity wasn't that odd, but there were some cases of people using it for fraud. Not that I intended any such thing.

"No, Miss Priscilla, the auction will be public, the winning bids the same. It will be simplicity itself for anyone to add them up and see what the result will be."

"I'm sure someone will."

"Enough now," said Simon. "Percival is a decent guy; no need to act like that." Simon stood up for me, telling her off. "You really should apologize."

"If after the event is over, you do as you say, I'll give you a full apology," she said to me, making me laugh and Simon sigh.

"You Shield folk sure are serious," I said, admiring her advocacy.

"I'm with the Lovers," she corrected.

"Ah, right. Can't say I've ever had much need of your Order's services," I demurred, having nearly forgotten about them.

"You might sometime; we do provide plenty. The marks are the most famous thing we do, and while you may not need pregnancy control, one would keep you from becoming a father unintentionally. Other than that, it's mostly dealing with marriages and women's issues, but there are a few other things for men we get involved in . . ."

"Wait, I thought the marks were only for girls?" I asked, confused.

Lover's Marks were the signature ability of the Lovers, a priestly order dedicated to just that. These marks were a form of birth control, some kind of tattoo or magical symbol. I wasn't overly familiar with the exact details because I'd never thought I'd need one, being completely incapable of getting pregnant.

"No, the variant for men is less common, but there is one."

"Might be wise to have . . ." I mumbled to myself, knowing from personal experience back on Earth that things could sometimes get out of hand. Luckily, I'd dodged the daddy bullet back then.

"Well, just come to the temple when you decide, and we'll be happy to help." It seemed my mumbling hadn't been nearly quiet enough.

"Understood."

CHAPTER 20

✱

MASQUERADE

The night of the party finally arrived, and I strolled into the ballroom, slipping on my mask. The one I'd made for myself was fanciful, white with feathers sticking out in all directions. Rowena was beside me and hers a pink version that matched perfectly with her dress.

"The guests are arriving," she observed as she looked out a window.

"Yes, shall we go and greet them?"

We moved from the window and around the room. Both sets of my grandparents were here, along with Rowena's parents as her chaperones. I'd not seen their masks until today, but each made sense. My grandfathers were wearing two opposite masks, one clearly militaristic, while the other looked decorated in cogs and small moving parts. My grandmothers, on the other hand, went for more understated masks, with geometric and floral designs etched in.

It was refreshing to see that they'd taken to the idea of a masked auction/ball so well. That had been my one worry, since I didn't know of any similar events; but apparently, half face masks were universal enough that the simple designs we'd put on the invitations had been enough to get the message across.

First to arrive were Simon and Priscilla. While his outfit was about what I expected, his date's mask was stark white, until you looked closer. A man and woman moved from each ear, nude and embracing in the center, a clear allusion to the Lovers. They greeted us briefly before continuing on.

More and more people showed up as the next hour or so passed, and I hated to admit it, but I didn't know or recognize all of them. Some I saw clearly, like Headmaster Logan, who couldn't hide his form or gruff voice. Others passed us, showing an invitation at the door, but happy to have fooled everyone as to whom they were. It was a masked party, after all, so I couldn't begrudge them that.

As I pulled back, letting people mingle as they would, my grandma approached me. Her perpetual displeased look was softened—practically a smile for her.

"This is going swimmingly," she said, looking over the crowd. "I'll admit, I worried when you described this to me, but you've managed it well. Perhaps something smaller next time though?" she questioned.

"I don't enjoy preparing these," I told her again, "and if I must, I'll be doing it how I please."

Rowena stifled a laugh, turning it into a sneeze behind me. I saw my grandma's eyes flit toward her and narrow, but they quickly returned to me. Really, it was lovely to see that my date was enjoying this conversation.

"When shall the main event begin?" Grandma asked acidly.

"After the dancing is done," I replied as placidly as I could.

At that moment, music started from one side of the hall, and the floor cleared, couples taking hands and moving toward the center. I, of course, chose to lead the charge, taking Rowena's and leaving my slightly displeased elder behind me. My date must have thought this was wonderful; she didn't hesitate a bit.

Normally, it was considered inappropriate to dance with the same woman too much, but seeing as Rowena and I were courting, there was much more leeway. After several dances with her, we did have to move to other partners though. Everyone split, moving to others. Several of the women I danced with were unknown to me that night, a few whispering small jokes as we parted and winking. It was a time to let things get a bit wilder, seeing as nobody knew who they were.

"It's been a pleasure, young man, and one of such good pedigree. I long to see what you've brought us tonight," one said as she flitted away into the crowd. I tried to catch a better glance at her but couldn't. Before the auction officially began, a representative from the Order of the Shield rose to the platform. Getting him here had been something of a coup on my part, but with what we were doing, he didn't argue.

"Greetings, ladies and gentlemen," the man said from beneath a plain mask bearing nothing but a shield on one cheek, "and thank you all for coming. Tonight you'll be bidding on items sold for the express purpose of benefiting our local orphanage. Some of you have certainly recognized me, some of you haven't, but know that I am here to ensure that all funds are taken where they should be, with all proceeds going directly to the children. So, please allow me to open the night."

Most of the items were of little repute—heaters, coolers, items that played gentle tunes or made soft light. I'd seen to it that each was artistic and well made, but they weren't special. They all sold well, though, each bringing several times what they were worth. Of course, this was a time for nobles to show off, to give to something worthwhile while getting a pretty trinket they could talk about later.

The last item, however, was something from my personal donation—one of my toy planes. The bidding started low, but soon exploded beyond reason. Several of the people here seemed determined to have it. Fifty gold coins, then a hundred, two. It kept climbing until even the auctioneer began to look nervous. However, one by one the bidders reached their limits. When only two remained, I could clearly see who they were.

"Two-seventy-five," a man said. He stood by the strange girl I'd been dancing with earlier.

His opponent, whom I recognized as Mr. Ignus, shook his head, clearly displeased. Well, he would get over it. It wasn't like he couldn't request one of those from me. Not sure I'd have sold him one, but we could have at least had the discussion.

As the night ended and the guests received their items, he approached me.

"You, me, somewhere private, now."

"This way," I led him to the second floor, abandoned for this event and used only for storage.

"Do you not have any sense?" he asked as we reached an empty hallway.

"What?" I asked. "I didn't sell any guns or anything." I'd considered it but pulled them out at the last minute, knowing someone might have issues.

"That model you sold. What were you thinking? I'll assume it works because I know you. Do you know how dangerous a working example of a flying machine would be? The tactical advantage alone is absolutely insane. Goodness, I knew you were working on the full-sized one, but not that you'd sell your work so easily."

As he was ranting, my ears picked up something else—a feminine voice, one that pinged in my memory, though I couldn't place it and focus on him at the same time.

"Come on, you asshole, just get in! Yes, yes, get your box, and that bitch . . . There you go, I'll teach you a lesson you won't forget." It was faint, from a hallway or two over.

"Hold it, wait," I said to Ignus. "There's something."

"Got you," the voice said, and Ignus yelled, reaching toward his left ear.

A *BOOM* shook the windows as the lawman reached up, pulling out an earpiece and tossing it away. I could briefly hear it screaming in a high-pitched tone.

"Attack!" he yelled, and I turned, running toward where I'd heard the voice.

It clicked as I rounded the corner and saw her there. The smallish goblin girl in her massive goggles stood by a window, something that looked like a detonator switch in her hand.

"You," I seethed, pulling out the gun I'd been keeping with me constantly.

"Me? You? What are you doing here?" she asked, clearly surprised.

CHAPTER 21

★

TROUNCED

"What are you doing here?" the goblin girl asked, goggles flashing in the low light.

I didn't bother trying to talk, instead drawing the pistol I'd taken to carrying on me at all times. I'd heard her words, I'd heard the explosion. Someone was almost certainly dead, and this wasn't the time for talking.

She was quick, too, her hand flashing upward a beat after my own. It wasn't superhuman speed like I had, just good reactions. As my finger squeezed the trigger, a blue glow surrounded my weapon. I could see as the gun fell, almost in slow motion, but couldn't do anything about it. Clearly she was up to something.

The weapon exploded, some kind of blockage from her magic—small, exact, and incredibly fast. It looked almost like something out of an old cartoon, with the barrel bursting and curling away. As it did, a piece of shrapnel sliced across my bicep, another catching the edge of my cheek and leaving a deep score.

"Now, now, I've seen that trick enough times," she chided as I recoiled, the pain from the blast radiating across me. "You didn't think it'd work again, did you?"

"Honestly, I was kind of hoping," I said as I threw the now broken weapon at her, at a loss for what else to do with it.

"Come now, don't you have something new?" she said, the shards of the gun stopping and hovering in place.

"Still working on it," I admitted as I charged and threw my hardest punch at her, only for it to be intercepted by one of her bubble shields.

"Shame, you do have such interesting toys. However, I'm not here for you."

She'd seen my tricks, but I'd also seen hers, and when her goggles shifted I closed my eyes. The flash was visible even through my eyelids, but not nearly as disabling as it had been last time. Her follow-up with a force wave that sent me sprawling into a nearby wall didn't miss though.

"I'll stop you," I wheezed as I tried to catch my breath and rise.

The rubble around me picked me up once more and slammed me back down.

"Kindly stop. Big Sister likes you as much as she can like a human, and I think she'd be peeved if I have to kill you. Like I said, I'm not here for you."

"If you don't mind my asking, who are you here for then?" came a familiar voice.

Ignus had caught up and looked almost calm as he stood in the hallway, hands at his sides, eyes flicking between me and the girl.

"The ones who've been killing my brothers and sisters. Who are you?" she asked him.

"Ah, you may call me Ignus. I'll admit, it is refreshing to speak with one of your kind. We've had such trouble—"

"We?" she asked.

"Ah, I represent the authorities of this city. I believe we might be able to solve all of this peacefully. Though my people have been looking for yours. To my knowledge none have managed direct contact so far."

He was so calm I wanted to smack him. I was lying here, out of breath and cut up, and he was having a polite conversation like they were meeting in a park or something. I wasn't fool enough to interrupt while they spoke though. He seemed to be up to something.

"Interesting, I'll relay your intent upward," Greta said, ears perking. "But for now I must go."

I didn't need to guess at why either; I could hear it. There were other noises from down below. Commotion, a lot of it. Yelling, not screaming in fear, but something to be sure. Ignus didn't try to do anything as the goblin girl retreated, bouncing down the hall at speed.

"What was that?" I asked as I tried to rise from the rubble.

"Building rapport," he said. "You did indicate that not all of them were mad, didn't you? And if I'm not much mistaken, that was one of the goblins you've interacted with before?"

"It is," I admitted. "She was there when—"

"Yes, I know. Also, what was I supposed to do? She soundly defeated you, and I don't have the capability to defeat her while she's on her guard. Next time maybe don't rush in."

"Next time I need to be better prepared," I grumbled.

"Agreed, and better trained." As he spoke, I shot him a look that I hope communicated the fact that had my gun not been broken, it wouldn't be the only thing I'd have shot at him.

"Enough of that, we need to check on the others."

It took me a moment to check myself before we headed downstairs. I was weaponless, Ignus was powerless, and frankly, neither of us had come prepped for battle, but that didn't mean we got to run away. No, regardless of the situation, we needed to move forward, to continue toward the danger, for that is the path both of us had chosen.

The smell hit me like a hammer as we entered the main hall. Most of my people had run off, but not all of them. Simon, Priscilla, the priest from the Shield. They were here, as well as my and Rowena's families. Most of them were sprawled on the ground, retching, pale, but seemingly unharmed. A few of the men were pulling themselves together but were clearly spattered with vomit.

Only one person wasn't—the proprietor, who lay still among the chaos. I recognized his suit. His head was gone, melted by the looks of it. There was no blood, but that didn't detract from the fact that he was seriously dead.

"But why?" I asked, confused at the one dead person in the room. As far as I knew he hadn't even been a threat.

"We need to find out," Ignus muttered.

Priscilla rose on shaky legs, stumbling as she tried to help the others up. By the time I made it over to her it was clear that both she and the other priest were in a minor panic.

"Death priest?" she asked the elder caster.

"He didn't kill us, but we need to report this and now," the man said with a shake of his head.

"Are you okay?" I asked when I reached them.

"No, no, we're not," Priscilla said. "That was clearly an unauthorized use of offensive priestly magic. I'd heard that perhaps there was someone, but that wasn't even a human, was it?"

"Probably not," I admitted.

"People need to know, the right people, right now." That was all she had to say before seeing to the others.

CHAPTER 22

★

INVESTIGATORS

I learned a few things over the next several hours.

Firstly, though according to history books, the various Orders had declined in power a bit from their peak, it didn't mean they were weak. Two priests letting it slip that there was a death priest on the loose meant that there was now a lot of scrutiny. I wasn't sure what that would mean, but both Priscilla and her companion wanted a full breakdown from me on what I knew.

Secondly, it looked like Ignus and his people might have downplayed the danger to these same Orders. Perhaps someone somewhere knew exactly what was going on, but it appeared the local leadership was now fully up in arms about the appearance of a rogue, non-human priest. The fact that he seemed so willing to kill and disable alarmed them as well.

"So that's your story, young man?" asked the priest, who'd come to see me whilst we were still cleaning everything up. His name was Father Leerson, and his eyes were sharply focused on me.

"Yes, sir," I answered. He looked less like a priest and more like an inquisitor.

"You knew about these creatures, about their leader?" he asked, accusingly.

"I did, and I reported that information to the proper authorities." I was a bit irritated at his tone.

"So you did, so you did," he said with a small placating gesture. "It really should have been reported to us though . . . I don't suppose you know why it wasn't?"

"You would have to ask the duke and his men," I responded.

"And I shall. We were told of certain deaths, certain . . . incidents, but not of all the details, clearly."

"I was there for what happened with the archmage. You don't need to hide it from me," I told him bluntly.

"Interesting."

"As was one of these creatures, the one who I suspect was responsible for the bomb." I could lie to him, or hide it, but I really had no need to at this point. More secrecy would probably just piss these people off, and I knew well enough from my studies what an angry biomancer could do, for that is what the priests were, regardless of what they claimed.

"Very interesting." He thought for a few moments. "And, if I might ask, what is your opinion of this *father*, the one we suspect of this incident."

"He's insane," I told him bluntly. "Dangerously, vigorously insane. Some of the others of his kind may not be though."

"Oh? What makes you say that?"

"I've talked to them, and the one I fought could easily have slain me, but she didn't."

"A quirk of their psychology, perhaps?"

"No, they seem like us. I've spoken to a few of them; some at least seem reasonable. Even if I'm not seeing all of the pieces, there's something more going on."

"On that I can certainly agree."

"What will you do if you find them?" I asked him, curious as to how they would handle the situation.

"Well, the leader here may or may not be a death priest. If he is, he must be killed; but, if he isn't, and is possible to reason with, we may try to communicate." At my raised eyebrow he went on. "The Orders aren't opposed to other races by any dogma. In fact, we welcome elves without any issue at all. Few join, but that's neither here nor there."

It was so weird to me how some, but not all, of the sayings in English translated over. Evidence of others like me was my guess.

"I've a question, if you don't mind," I said.

"Certainly, though I cannot promise an answer."

"What exactly is a death priest? I've heard the term a few times now, but I'm unfamiliar with it."

"Ah, not something one runs into unless they study our particular history and arts, I suppose. Very well then, a death priest is a priest, but one who has gone completely mad. Normally this manifests in killing everything around them, hence the name. They are formidable opponents, as one might suspect, and luckily, quite rare. Something about our magic seems to engender a certain desire to do right."

"I see, then you should know that Father thinks he's doing right," I told him.

"How so?" he asked.

"I spoke to him, briefly. I believe he's trying to *improve* people, though he doesn't seem to care how many he must kill for those improvements to come to fruition."

"That is concerning, and dangerous. Not what I feared, but in some ways . . ."

"Yes," I said, nodding.

"Don't suppose you might shed some light on why they were here tonight, or killing these people?"

"I've already told you that I don't know that," I said, a bit frustrated at that repeated question. He'd asked about five times, all in different ways.

At this point, Ignus decided to enter the small side room we'd taken up. He looked none too pleased.

"This young man has been aiding me in my work, and he is well outside your authority," he said, sounding quite peeved.

"With the facts we've seen, I care to disagree."

"Disagree all you like, but it remains so. My people are taking up the investigation, as we have been for some time."

"This matter concerns a rogue priest, and it's clearly our jurisdiction," Father Leerson said with a frown.

"A non-human invader is mine."

"Not when they're using priest magic."

"Ladies, you're both pretty," I interjected, "but perhaps it would be better if you worked together?"

They both looked at me slightly aghast. It seemed that one hadn't made the rounds yet. I wanted them working together. Perhaps the priestly faction had fallen out of favor, but they still had people, and power. Those Orders of theirs were international and might well be able to get information we couldn't here. Similarly, Ignus and his people knew this city better than anyone.

"We're not giving up an ongoing investigation to an outside entity," the lawman huffed.

"Nor are we giving up what is clearly our area of expertise."

"Both of you want answers. Perhaps you should allow the other to help. Ignus here knows more about what's going on than any of us." The man in question looked peeved I'd brought that up. "And I'm sure that the number of priests the good Father here could bring in would certainly be of help examining the bodies." The priest looked irritated that I was implying he aid Ignus.

"And when it comes to dealing justice?" Father Leerson asked.

"I think everyone agrees at least that their leader needs to die. Start there." That at least got me a pair of guffaws. There was hope for them yet.

CHAPTER 23

TARGETS AND ADVANCEMENTS

Ignus may have come to get me, but he was now distracted. This was a good opportunity to make my escape, so I left the two investigators to their deepening discussion and slipped out. I was heading back into the building proper to see who was where and how they were. Several people I recognized were sitting in the main hall—primarily, both sets of my grandparents; Rowena; and Lucas, whom I'd only seen at the beginning of the night; along with Simon and Priscilla.

"Thank goodness you're all right," my paternal grandmother said.

"Of course he is dear," her husband said, reassuringly. "He was with a priest."

Before the others could get going I decided to speak up.

"Yes, I'm fine, perfectly fine. What's the damage though? I felt that explosion, so don't bother telling me everyone is unharmed."

"One of the carts blew up," Lucas said. "Looks like it was only the one, though, and thankfully nobody but the driver and passengers were near it. That bastard goblin also only killed the proprietor."

"Any clue on why he did that?" I asked, looking at each of them. There were sighs. I was guessing everyone else had asked that too.

"No, but it was targeted," Simon answered.

"You're sure?"

"Very, he went straight for the man. We were just in the way. If he'd wanted to kill us, he probably could have, since none of us were prepared for the fight."

"Yes, I'm going to need to make some preparations, I think," I said. "I'll understand if you don't want to spend too much time around me, with this now happening."

"I'm sorry, my friend, but I'm afraid you're correct," Simon replied, and both Lucas and I were taken aback. Even his girlfriend looked shocked. Sure, I'd offered the warning, but I'd not expected him to heed it.

"Simon!" Priscilla said.

"No, this danger is real, and I have people to look after. I have siblings, family, other friends, and you. If this problem were within my abilities, it would be one thing, but it isn't. I'll not be getting involved in this any further."

Priscilla looked like she wanted to argue as he took her hand and began to lead her to the door. I didn't though. Sure, his move had been unexpected, but he was right. We were all well out of our depths here. These problems were also finding me like a magnet, so keeping his distance wasn't something I could really blame him for.

I could see Lucas' eyes hardening as he watched our friend go. He seemed to take Simon's departure harder than I had, but perhaps it was his age. At that age I'd been the ride-or-die type, too, but had I known what that meant? No. Nor had I really thought of what it would do to those around me, too caught up in my own mind to consider the effects of what I was doing.

"Don't even say it," Lucas said without looking at me. "You're one of my people, and I'm here." His sister giggled under her breath but nodded as I looked to her as well.

"That boy is responsible, but the three of you aren't here for anything except learning," my grandpa said in a gruff voice. "You're not to go looking for trouble. Am I clear?"

"Grandpa," I said, turning to him. "I never go looking for it; it just seems to find me." That got me a huff of laughter.

"All this talk," Grandma said. "You boys need to calm yourselves and let the authorities take care of it. Now, come along, it's already late and we should all head home. Lucas, do you and your sister have an escort?"

"Yes, ma'am," replied Lucas.

"Then be about it. It's time to leave."

Over the next few days, I found some benefits to that night's activities. My family was no longer pressuring me to put on events, which was a huge win. I also had a bit more personal time to work on my projects. People avoiding me was something that I would never take for granted.

My primary project was to finish the first level of my core. These cores had been how Simon had been helping me make magical objects, and with his keeping me at arm's reach I would need to finish my own. At first I'd been concerned that this would be a trial, needing to use the rooms at my school to aid in the meditation practice, but that was a non-issue.

"Just use the one in the house," Mrs. Rider had told me when I'd griped about it.

I hadn't known, but apparently, most large houses kept a designated room for this advancement on hand, and the reason for this was twofold. First, there were situations, like the one I was in now, where a young member of the family would need to work on forming the first level of their core. Second, there were also the servants who had minor magics to consider. These "talents," as they were sometimes called, could also form a core, though at a much slower rate. Having a dedicated space for people to advance their abilities inside the home meant they wouldn't spend as much time away, and it boosted the power of the staff as a whole.

The room in question was one I'd never much cared to look at. It was by the laundry, of all things, tucked in one of the areas between where the servants were most of the time and where the family lived. I'd always assumed it was some kind of storage space, and though there were boxes, the outline on the ground told me the tool that was here was working well. Mrs. Rider guided me in, and we found that we weren't alone.

Kaylee sat in the center of the small circle, sweat beading on her brow as she worked on the same thing I had been planning to. After a few seconds her eyes fluttered open and she started, seeing us there before her.

"Oh, my apologies! I didn't know you needed to use—"

"It's fine. I wasn't going to at the moment anyway," I lied, not wanting to interrupt one of the few paths toward power she had.

"Actually, I was done for today, my lord. I'm not able to do much . . ." I gave her a reassuring smile as she spoke.

Over the next week I passed by periodically, using my enhanced senses to check and see if she was there before going in. Perhaps I was a sucker for her, but what else should a big brother be? No, that was proper. She was there a lot, too, and never for very long, as she had almost no mana, but several times a day, presumably, when her power recovered.

When she wasn't using it, I was. Even if I'd been a bit reserved on this particular exercise while in school, I'd still made progress. The meditation took me into a state where I could see connections, looking almost like circuits, and I put them together in an orderly way. It was intuitive, slow, and easy to tell when it was right or wrong. With the time I could put toward it, I made massive progress too. Before I realized it, I was on the last little bit, pushing with my mind and magic to form the final connection.

There was a surge and a tingling in my head, as much as I could feel something like that when I was in this state. Then, before me appeared a set of words, words I'd seen before and ones that told me the original maker of this core item was from my world. There, in plain English, letters formed, the old words, the old joke. Ones even those who only ever played with programming knew.

"Hello, World!"

CHAPTER 24

✱

TRINKETS

"Hello, World!"

Yes, that old archmage and the insane goblin weren't the only ones like me. She'd known, and I'd known on some level, but there it was. It was confirmation that I was now seeing for myself a clear message to those of us who came after. Sadly, it didn't tell me everything. There were still so many questions.

Why? Why had we been pulled into this world? Why had we been chosen, if chosen we were? Was there some greater meaning to all of this? I didn't know, nor did I know who could answer these questions yet. Perhaps nobody could. Perhaps none knew for sure the reasons or methods, or perhaps they did. In the end it was just curiosity, as the answers were unlikely to help with my real problems.

No, it was better to focus on the things I could do, and needed to do now. One of those, now that my core was finished, was to begin making items again, but not just any items. I needed defenses, offenses, protections for people and places, and all the best.

Some of these I couldn't manage right now; not because I didn't want to, of course, but because there were some stark limits on what I could do with the first level of the core. The higher core levels would allow more complex spells, the sort of things that would be best for difficult applications, but even this one was useful. I already had a book of basic offenses. Our class on the subject covered some by necessity—simple elemental attacks, force applications. Most of these wouldn't be as good as a modern weapon, but there would be some variety that I could add, variety I badly needed.

Defenses were a little harder, as they were by nature complicated. I could at the very least make a few basic shielding items. Their potency would be minor, but they would be better than nothing. Something like a basic shield should be able to stop a bullet or two before the mana within ran out; though I doubted I'd get much more than that.

Vehicles would come soon too. I already had the runic scripts for those, after all, and none of what we were using was particularly complex. It might take a while to create one that could hold the amount of mana I'd need for any long flights, but I could, in theory, do it on my own.

I walked out of the room and into my workshop, a spring in my step. The staff seemed to keep out of the way, preferring to remain unseen for the most part. A lot of household workers were like that, keeping hidden while they did their work. With my senses I could hear every person within thirty feet or so, identify each one by their footsteps. I knew which maid was where, when they ducked into rooms as I approached, and where the butlers were.

My shop had been prepared with a few items for me to enchant. They weren't anything more than basic pieces. Making an item was different than I thought it would be, more meditative, almost pleasant. Perhaps for some it would be boring, but it seemed to me almost like machining itself, the exactness and timing, letting the world flow around me.

My first piece was nothing to brag about—a simple shield charm, held in an unadorned bracelet. The runes were hidden on the inside, ready to charge. It still took me a few hours to make, but it had a purpose. After a brief test I left it to the side, fully charged.

Then I went about a second piece; this time a weapon. Rather than make anything through the magical tools, I turned toward my shop. Turning a small metal wand was easy as pie. People had made these as toys for children after that certain series of books, and while mine was made of a low quality silver alloy rather than wood, it took on a similar shape. Adding a simple fire-bolt type spell to it was no trouble either.

I went over the metals I had, looking closely at each as I considered other projects. It was a well-known fact that certain materials tended to be better for enchantment than others. Metals were better than anything that didn't come from a magical creature, as far as I knew, and among them there was a hierarchy.

It followed closely with electrical conducting properties; not exactly, but close enough for my work. Gold and silver were, of course, the best metals to use; though, they were incredibly expensive. Aluminum was, too, but I'd only seen and heard of a few used pieces, all called sky-metal by the natives. It, too, was an incredibly rare substance. Silver and its alloys were the go-to for most people, and would do for me.

"Lord Percival, it's nearly time for supper," came a small call from the doorway.

I looked up to see Kaylee standing framed by the portal. She was always the one sent for me because of how much the staff knew I preferred her over others. I really didn't like being disturbed, but with her I couldn't bring myself to be even a bit peeved about it.

"Actually, I was hoping to see you, Kaylee. Could you come here for a moment?"

"Did you need something, sir?" she asked as she stepped inside, looking at the room. Nobody but me cleaned this room, and it showed. It was far dustier than the rest of the house.

"Yes, take these. I'll get around to making some for the rest of the staff who can use magic, but with current events, it would make me far more comfortable should some of our people have a way to protect themselves if the worst should come to pass."

She looked at the two items on the table, eyes bulging. "My lord, I don't have the money for something like that..."

"Consider them part of your uniform then. We pay for those..." I mumbled the last part, actually unsure.

"You do not, Lord Percival," she corrected quietly.

"Regardless, we still need staff who have at least something should the worst come to pass. These are for emergencies only though. You're to run should something happen. Understand? I'll explain how they work." And, I did, briefly. There really wasn't much to it. Point the wand and focus or push a bit of mana into the bracelet to activate a several-foot-wide shield.

"I..." she began.

"It is the job of the strong to protect the weak," I said, not quite quoting an old ruler, "and the duty of those in power to shield those under them. So take them, please." As I spoke I pushed the items into her hand and turned, leaving the room.

As I left, I clenched my jaw. I was a coward for not telling her the whole truth, that I gave her those because of who she was, because as her brother, half or not, it was my duty to keep her safe. What if I did though? Could I actually change anything for her for the better? No, no I couldn't. Not yet, not until I gained real power. I would gain that power though. Enough one day to tell her the truth, to make people accept her as they should. Until then, this was the very least I could do.

CHAPTER 25

✱

GAMES GIRLS PLAY

It took a couple of weeks, but someone eventually did invite me to another party. Now, the issue wasn't that I was some kind of social pariah. Quite the opposite, actually. It was that nobody was having any gatherings. Since the last one had ended in the death of the owner of the venue and a couple of the guests, it was quite the wet blanket on the seasonal soirees.

Then again, it was carte blanche for the gossip mill, who were in full swing. I wasn't even in on that particular group as well I might have been, but I was still hearing about it. For one, those two had bought items at the event, but nobody knew who they were. Well, the authorities might have, but they weren't sharing. In fact, these buyers weren't on any of the guest lists, nor were any of the known guests hurt in the explosion.

Personally, I'd thought they were some couple who was either very good at hiding their identities or connected to one of my friends somehow. That, however, proved to be untrue, as Ignus' people had come around asking about them. The fact that nobody had any answers was likely vexing for him, but for the ladies around town who liked to spread rumors, it was a full-on holiday.

All of these same ladies wanted me to come and give them my account, too, or at least be around to hear it. Everyone who'd been there had a story to tell, even if most of them had left before the explosion; and, being that I was there and had even fought one of the attackers, they were champing at the bit to hear what I had to say. The only reason people hadn't started showing up at my house, aside from the formidable defenses installed by my kin, was the fact that it would be socially unacceptable to do so.

Similarly, the secret about goblins in town was now completely blown. Rumors had been building for some time, but they were just that, and disregarded as such. Now, however, multiple priests had been present when one of the beasts showed up, attacking them and killing a man. Those priests were pissed beyond recognition that they'd not been informed of the danger and were making sure everyone who was anyone was hearing about it.

"Percival, I'd like you to join my aunt for an event at her home in a few days," Rowena said during one of our periodic study sessions.

"And why is that?" I asked.

"Because she's pestering me endlessly about it, about that whole debacle. She's insisting she hear the story that I've already told her again and again, and I'd like you to get her to leave me be."

"I think me telling your aunt to silence herself wouldn't help," I pointed out.

"Boys," she scoffed. "No, I've not even told her to shut up; I just want her to."

"If you haven't told her, how is she supposed to know?" I asked.

"She just is, and she does. She's not stupid, well, *that* stupid. Anyway, if you come and give her what she wants, she'll be happy and leave me be. She's been asking about you a lot, too, and I think that's what she actually wants."

"If that's what she wants, why doesn't she just ask? It's not like I'm particularly busy, and she knows our relationship. It wouldn't be odd at all for her to meet with me. Goodness, she could even frame it as checking in on your potential future husband or something." Girls really did like to beat around the bush, a little too much for my liking; and if her aunt had just talked to me, this whole thing would have been simple beyond belief.

She sighed, looking exceedingly tired. "It's not the same, Percival, and it wouldn't get you to her home telling the story, where she could be the center of attention. If you don't want to go, you don't have to."

That was both a lie and a landmine, and we both knew it. Perhaps I wasn't the best when it came to dealing with women, in either world, at any age, but I saw this for what it was.

"Rowena, I didn't say I wouldn't go; I will. I just wanted to know why she wouldn't come to me and instead bothered you. Wouldn't it be better if people didn't do that in the future?" I tried to speak calmly, but it wasn't doing much good.

"They will come to me, because... You just don't get it," she huffed.

"No, I don't, but I don't want people pestering you rather than pestering me. Is there anything I can do to stop that?"

It wasn't untrue either. There were layers of social interaction, particularly among women, that I really didn't get. Noblewomen seemed to make the girls of my previous world look straightforward by comparison, so that didn't help. They liked their games, and for some reason, I thought they got satisfaction from playing them, even if I couldn't figure out why.

"There isn't," she replied. "It's all about... making things happen. If she comes to you, it means she had to, not that she wanted to. How many women in this city could make that happen? Most of them, I imagine. All of them in my family, even more as well. She wants you to come, but she does not want to be seen wanting you to come. She gets the credit for you showing up, without appearing to make you show up. It's like you want to be there—the first place you go to tell your story; it would be to her."

"Then maybe I shouldn't? I mean, wouldn't that be a display of power? We could go somewhere else first, take that from her, and make her think about being such a nuisance in the future," I suggested.

Rowena took a full five seconds to pick up a piece of paper, roll it into a tube, and smack my head with it like I was a naughty dog.

"How do you think she'd respond to that exactly, Percival? Poorly, I can assure you, and she's my aunt. If she gets it in her head to do so, she can easily make the minor irritation she's been so far look like a cute little pout. She's known much of my family much longer than I have and has her talons in them too. She wants something simple and *will* go about making me a pariah in our family if I'm a contrarian about it. If I snub her just because, she'd take every chance she could for years to do the same right back."

"That seems needlessly petty."

"No, it is the insistence upon proper decorum. You need lessons on it."

"Rowena, dear, my schedule for education is already packed full. I don't suppose I could impose on you to handle such matters for the time being?"

She actually laughed at that. Not much, but I'd take that over a scolding any day.

"That's exactly what I'm doing," she said, almost too sweetly.

"Then I'll trust your judgment. In the future, will you tell me about this though? I'd hate to step on someone's toes for no reason."

"Of course."

"Anything in particular I need to wear?" I asked.

"Actually . . ."

CHAPTER 26

✶

AUNTIE'S PARTY

Rowena's aunt lived on the outskirts of the more expensive districts in the city. Perhaps the man she'd married wasn't a titled noble, or he was lower on the totem pole than most I'd dealt with, or maybe she just liked it there. The area was closer to shopping and the roads leading out, so if she preferred to spend her time away from Exion rather than in it, this would be a pretty good spot.

Her house also didn't disappoint. It was not as grand as some of the mansions I'd seen, but really quite nice. The layout was similar to our own home—large interior, with clearly delineated space for the family and guests. I could even guess where the back passages were, and that was confirmed by the sounds of scurrying staff moving about as they tried to do their jobs with minimal interruption to the event itself.

"I'm so very glad you came," our host said with a smile.

"Well, it's been a while since last I got out, and Rowena suggested this might be a good place to work my way back into society properly after all the unpleasantness, Lady Emily," I said in response, giving credit where it was due and making sure she knew exactly why I'd come.

"Oh, she is such a dear, isn't she? How are you doing, though, after everything that happened?" It was funny, how she seemed so sympathetic, yet at the same time so very hungry for details.

"Not too badly, Lady Emily. I've seen these beasts before, of course."

"Please do tell, if it's not too much . . ."

"Of course," I obliged. "After all, people should know what's going on, shouldn't they?"

I spent the next several hours dictating some, but certainly not all, of my adventures and attacks against the goblins. The audience was rapt for it, too, with old men cheering as if fights were a jolly sport and ladies gasping at all the right moments. Of course, Rowena's aunt spent the whole time at the center of it all, pushing for more details.

"And what's that I heard about you saving some children from a monstrous bird?" one of the women asked, seemingly curious that I'd not brought it up.

"Oh, that? Didn't have anything to do with the goblins, as far as I know. I was just enjoying a day in the park when a man pointed it out. We never did find him though. Had he not said something, the poor little ones might well have died. Shame that I never got a chance to thank him. Odd fellow too."

"Odd how?" Lady Emily asked, leaning in.

"Well, his clothes, for one. He was wearing some kind of robe. More than that, his hair was pale white. Talked about how his daughter hated him getting out and about, so I think he may have been sickly or something."

"You know, I've volunteered in some of the hospitals about here," one of Rowena's other relatives chimed in. "If you could give a good description, perhaps I might find him?" People hummed and hawed sufficiently.

"How about I draw the fellow? I'm no expert artist, but I can sketch a bit," I offered.

Paper and a charcoal pencil soon made their way into my hands. It was true, too, that I wasn't a master artist; nor was I particularly skilled at drawing faces, but I'd drawn enough diagrams over the years and made enough art that I could turn out something basic.

"No, don't know him," the woman who'd spurred the idea said with a shrug.

That was that, then, and I left the drawing sitting there. We'd had dinner, and after a brief time mingling together, it was time for the men and women to split for evening activities.

"Ah, my boy, thank you for entertaining my wife so," Rowena's uncle said to me after we'd left the ladies to adjourn to the smoking room. "You've no idea how much she's enjoyed this. Been digging into everything she can about that horrid incident."

"No need, sir, but please do keep her from digging too deeply. Those monsters are not to be trifled with. They've already killed, and I'd like to see that they don't harm anyone else."

"Haha, I'll make sure to increase the wards on the house then. Can't hurt, and they're a bit dated as it is. Wouldn't worry too much though. She's not going to go poking around any sewers; she just interrogates the men who do," he assured me.

"Are they truly that dangerous?" one of the other men asked.

"They've got magic," I said. "At least the ones I've seen do. Would you underestimate any mage?"

"No, surely not," the man said, solemnly.

"Luckily, it doesn't look like they've got enchanted items, though, so there's that."

They smoked, or at least many of them did, though I abstained. Never liked that habit; the smell was enough for me. I did partake in a little brandy though. Just a little. The flavors danced, enhanced perhaps by my stronger senses, or it was just that good. These men were wealthier than I'd been on Earth, of course, so most of the food that we had was top quality.

Parties didn't go on forever, so soon enough the time came for us all to bid one another goodnight. Rowena joined me in the main room once more, looking pleased enough that I doubted she hadn't gotten something out of all this.

As we were leaving she stopped, looking down at the picture I drew.

"Do you know him?" I asked, watching her furrow her brow.

"I don't think so, but he's horribly familiar," she said, sounding a tad bothered. "Would you mind if I took this?" she asked her aunt.

"No, dear, so long as you tell me should you find him," her aunt said with a hint of mischief in her voice.

"Very well," Rowena said, folding the paper and putting it in her bag.

"So, he's familiar?" I asked as we settled into the carriage, which would take each of us to our respective homes, hers first, of course.

"Yes, but I can't place him. It's quite vexing." She gave a little pout.

"Ah, well if you do, I'd like to thank him," I said with a shrug.

"Hmm, yes."

CHAPTER 27

✶

NEW SCHEDULE

All things have to come to an end, and my winter vacation was no different. Before I knew it, the time had come to pack my things and return to school, and the stress and time crunch that always seemed to follow me there. I hated that. Even if I liked the place, it was just too much. Even if I was being excluded from a few things as my years progressed, I certainly wasn't getting any more time.

Several of the staff waited as I boarded the carriage that would take me back to what was more accurately becoming my home. All stood at attention, smiling and giving their quiet goodbyes. Among them Kaylee, her little shield charm and wand tucked away in her uniform. I could almost feel them, almost notice the magic I'd made, which was something totally new to me. It was a sense like something was there, but not an answer to what and difficult to accurately describe. It was more like a smell or a sensation on the back of my neck. A couple others had them, too, and as if by instinct, I could tell who didn't have theirs on them.

My little half-sister had tried to refuse my gift, stating it was too much for a master to give to a servant. She'd pouted adorably and held back, but when it became clear all of our magic-capable staff were getting them, she relented. She was right, of course. It was far too valuable a gift to pass off to the help, but I wasn't going to leave her undefended, even if that meant I had to defend others too.

Cobblestones clattered under wheels as I slowly made my way down the path. The sound was oddly calming, rhythmic, and soon I felt myself drifting off to sleep. The journey wasn't too long, as we were going just outside the walls, but it was enough for me to catch a quick nap.

I was stirred awake when we arrived, but that had been expected, so I suppose I could forgive the world for not accommodating my whims. My eyes fluttered as we slowed, body sensing the change in pace.

No sooner had we stopped than a younger student ran up to us. He had a letter in hand.

"You can't be serious," I said flatly.

"You're Percival, right?" he asked.

"Yes."

"This is for you from the headmaster," the kid said, holding out the paper.

Had I ever been like him? He looked like just a child. With a sigh I took the letter, flipping it open and reading it before sighing again.

My walk to Headmaster Logan's office was well practiced. I knew where to go, which halls were best or worst to go down, even the proper way to get a good view as I did so. I really needed to stop coming here; it never ended well.

"Ah, you've finally arrived," the bear of a man said as I entered. "Sit, join us."

Joining us, as he often did when I ended up in trouble, was Sir Kendrick, the man assigned by the king to make sure I was properly trained. The knight nodded to a chair nearby, where I sat. I found the seat pleasant, comforting, familiar.

"Sir, I didn't even make it out of my carriage," I said. "That must be some sort of record."

"No lip, lad, and it isn't. The current recordholder was visited two weeks into his vacation for discipline. Managed to disgrace the school publicly and got the correction he needed immediately."

"Hate to be him," I said.

"No, I think I turned out fairly well once I got my head on straight. I've some hope you will too. Enough chatter though. We're not here for that."

That was a surprise, and an insight into the headmaster's life I didn't think I'd ever get. To think he'd been a rulebreaker in his youth, the man who seemed to want nothing more than to beat us into soldier-shaped molds. It had me blinking wildly for a solid five seconds.

"Attention, Percival," Sir Kendrick said, bringing me back to the here and now.

"I've been thinking about your training," began Headmaster Logan.

Oh shit.

"And the results we've gotten. They're acceptable, but I've considered things. How would you like to take less classes?"

"I feel like something's going to be added to that, sir," I pointed out.

The man scoffed under his breath, just enough for me to hear.

"Indeed, you see your grades and work are good enough that we could excuse you from physical participation in a number of subjects, and your professors agree. You'd still need to do the assignments, but you'd do them on your own. Additionally I'd be asking our good knight here to oversee some particular training for you personally."

"With all due respect, I'm not sure more combat training would be overly productive. I already do quite a bit."

"No, not swordsmanship, tactics, or even the guns you seem so fond of," Sir Kendrick answered. "I would be training you in magical resistance. Your most recent encounter shows you need it, and it will give you an edge against enemies. Normally, we hold off on this until your final year of education, and even then, it is not a core subject but one left for future mastery. You would join me in mastering the art as well as you can instead."

Thinking only took a few seconds. Most of my classes were still something along the lines of high-school level, not particularly difficult with my slightly better memory in this life. I'd already done most of this once, so doing things like math and basic writing was horribly boring. This, though, would give me something useful and clear out some of my schedule at the same time.

My thoughts flicked back to the little goblin wizard and her goggles. She kept blitzing me with magic, magic I didn't know how to fight against. If I'd had resistance, well, then we might be able to do something about that. She'd even pointed out that I needed more tricks, so more tricks she would get.

"I think I would like that," I agreed.

"Good, here is your schedule for the year then," the headmaster said, passing me a sheet of paper. Nearly all of my classes, excluding combat training, were replaced with a mixture of personal study time and training schedules with Sir Kendrick. It was an intensive regimen he had planned for me, but he was a knight in service to the monarch, so I had to guess he knew his business. There was also an hour allotted each week to meet with each of the professors to go over my assignments, which I fully planned to do as fast as I could.

"We start tomorrow. Make sure to get some rest," Sir Kendrick said, smiling in a way that sent a chill down my spine.

CHAPTER 28

✷

MAGICAL RESISTANCE

I woke up, looking at the ceiling and knowing that the day would be magnificent. My mornings would be much the same of course, with breakfast first thing. Of course, waking up wasn't the hectic assembly it had been my first year, with our food being disturbed and work thrown off. No, it was as normal as a first day of school could ever be.

Older students looked tired, blinking and rubbing their eyes, and one or two asking friends to borrow materials they'd forgotten at home. Though I didn't participate, I was sure there was a thriving black market for such things. First year students were running around either unable to process the morning routine or so panicked that they looked like chickens with their heads cut off.

Food was good; filling, but simple. Nothing fancy adorned the table my friends and I sat at, but we had a good, filling bread, plenty of fruits and vegetables, some sausages, and porridge. We ate quickly, savoring the quick meal as best we could, knowing full well that these times could be cut short if the staff got a bee in their bonnets.

"Ready for Killic today?" asked a boy beside me.

"Don't have him—the headmaster reworked my schedule," I informed them.

"Seriously? How could they possibly fit anything else in there?" Lucas chimed in as he came to join us.

"Not more; less."

"How does that work?" the boy with the initial question asked. Everyone knew I was being put to the grindstone.

"I'm doing all the work on my own and studying privately with an instructor. I think I'll actually have free time," I told them.

Several boys patted my back, looking on with mock tears in their eyes.

"Oh, Percival, how you've changed, grown. You'll even get to live this year. That might be a first, seeing you out on anything but a rest day, not looking like you are in the middle of breaking yourself against your books," Lucas teased.

"Was I really that bad?" I asked.

"By the end of last year, your eyes were red every day, and I'm pretty sure you didn't comb your hair for a full week once," one of my dorm companions answered, munching a slice of apple.

"That's not true . . . I think," I said, trying to remember.

"Well, you looked better than Lucas there. He came back with his face all blue that one time, remember?" he asked.

I did, indeed. Lucas had been on the wrong end of a sparring match and managed to get himself actually hurt. He'd healed in a day or two, but it looked like his face had been smashed into a concrete wall for a while there.

"What happened with that anyway?" I asked.

"Snapped at the professor during a combat demonstration, and he introduced my face to the cobbles," Lucas replied. "Hurt a bit, but I learned a good trick out of it."

"Well," I said, looking at the people beginning to leave, "looks like it's time to head out."

As one, we rose and made our way to the doors. Lucas, who was in his final year, split off first, having a very different schedule than the rest of us. Only a few moments later, I had to break with the rest of my fellows as well, turning toward one of the smaller arena-like structures.

Sir Kendrick was there before I was, dressed in armor rather than his normal clothing.

"Good morning, Percival," he said. "Come in and let us begin."

"Sir, I'm still unclear as to what we're doing here," I said.

"Worry not; you'll be getting detailed instructions. This is one of the disciplines I had to master before joining His Majesty's service, so you'll have exactly what you need."

"Yes, sir," I answered with a nod.

"All people capable of magic naturally project an aura, as you well know. This is magic leaving the body, and relates to the level of our power. I'm told this is easier to explain to casters who can see such things, but it matters not. I have an aura, you have an aura, all of us. What we'll be doing is learning to control that aura."

"I'm not sure how that helps, sir?" I asked.

"By *pushing* outward you are able to fill the air around you with your own magic, which will resist the magic of others. This doesn't help against secondary effects, like a mage throwing a knife at you with magic, but it does against magic directly influencing you. There are a lot of factors, and it's not going to be mastered today, but you need to learn to do this, and when you do, hostile spells will flow around you like water flowing around a rock in a stream."

"Sounds like something we should teach earlier—"

"In the past it was, but it was decided that teaching schoolchildren to repel spells while they are still in the early stages is dangerous. A few incidents where one got angry and proved very difficult to restrain led to the change. Some youths still end up that way, though, stumbling upon the technique, or they're just so naturally gifted at it that they develop that way regardless."

That was true enough. All of us physical magic users seemed to develop a bit differently. My senses were far above par, though nowhere near the most extreme. Even at my strongest and fastest, I still fell behind Lucas, but I could hear and find people through walls, something I suspected he'd never been able to achieve. There were also a few people here and there who were like walking tanks, taking blows that would toss me like a leaf in the wind.

"Where do I start?" I asked.

The knight led me through a few meditative poses designed to put my body at ease. These were followed by exercises in which I would breathe in and out, trying to feel my mana, trying to focus it. None of that was fully foreign. My work with magical items was similar, but he started from the very basics, like this was the first time I'd touched on my internal power.

Inside me magic flowed, and while feeling it wasn't a strong sensation, there was a slight tingle where it moved, like static on my skin. Once I could feel it, Sir Kendrick had me focus it on one body part at a time. I had to increase the strength in my hands, or eyes, or ears, all little by little. This wasn't a terribly odd exercise, and worked sort of like learning to use my abilities again. Focusing my aura into my skin to harden it was an odd one, but it did give me a very slight boost.

"If you mastered that, you could temporarily boost your abilities in one way or another. Limited in use, and really more advanced than we're doing now, but we might work on it later. Generally, training to increase them permanently is better though."

Long-term gains came only from training, using our powers again and again and slowly building strength, not unlike normal physical exercise, only on another level. That was still interesting though—the idea of expanding one ability without weeks or years of effort would be worth it. For now, though, I got the feeling that outside of this very controlled exercise it would be difficult to pull off.

"Now onto our next part," the knight declared. "Grab your magic and push it to your skin. Don't bind it there, instead letting it flow."

I struggled to do what he said, but thought I was feeling it.

"How do I know if it worked?" I asked, straining.

To answer me, he pulled out a small rod from his belt and touched me with it. Instantly, a shock ran across my body, causing me to leap and lose concentration.

"Good, had you failed, you would not have been able to move at all. Not a bad start, young man," he told me with a smile.

"That rather hurt," I complained.

"Oh, come now, that was the lowest setting. Now sit back down, we've got a lot of work to do."

CHAPTER 29

✦

EXHAUSTION AMONG FRIENDS

I made it back to my dorm that evening somehow more tired than I'd have been if I'd gone to regular class. A few of the boys looked at me and, seeming to feel my mood, didn't bother me as I fell into bed.

While I wasn't having to go through the mental exercise, or even most of the physical, that didn't mean I wasn't putting forth effort. Despite the knight's assurances that eventually resistance would become second nature, it wasn't currently. Maintaining the pressure was a constant expenditure of will, interrupted by the constant shocks as he put my efforts through the ringer.

Even on the lowest setting the little taser baton Sir Kendrick was using could drop an unprepared man, and I suspected that if they weren't so mana-intensive, they'd make great additions to the police armaments. They hurt through my novice resistance, but I'd taken a shot or two with my guard down and knew it was far worse without it. That, at least, was some small light at the end of the tunnel—knowing that my efforts were doing something.

As I drifted in and out of sleep a knock came at my door.

"Come in."

Lucas appeared there, looking at me sprawled out still in my dirty clothes.

"Come now, Percival, at least wash before sleeping."

"You didn't have the day I had," I retorted.

"Perhaps not, but we must maintain some standard, however minimal."

"Is there a reason you came to bother me?"

"You didn't show up to dinner, and I was worried about you, my friend. Lucky I was, too, if you're this rough." As he spoke he took my chair, sitting down to watch as I didn't bother to rise.

"I'm informed you'll be getting some of the training I got today soon, since you're in your last year," I griped, hoping the threat would keep him from pushing too hard.

"Perhaps, and perhaps I'll be as poorly off as you are now."

"Not showing up to dinner hardly seems enough reason for all this," I pointed out, pulling myself onto my elbows. "What's the real reason?"

"Rowena asked me to keep an eye on you; she worries."

"Seriously?" I asked, blinking.

"She cares for you, in her own weird way, but she does. She's also perceptive enough to know you've been pushing yourself to your absolute limits, and you're getting worse."

"This whole plan was supposed to push me back to a reasonable schedule," I said with a sigh. "Now I'm missing meals and barely able to walk."

"At least you know it though. Percival, I want you to promise me something."

"What's that?" I wasn't agreeing to anything until I'd heard it.

"Take care of yourself, and listen to people. You don't have enough people looking out for you, and next year I won't be here. Maybe Simon could've helped, but he walked away, the bastard."

"No, he wasn't wrong for that. Being near me is a danger right now, and he has his own people to look out for."

Lucas looked like he wanted to disagree but held his tongue. I was glad for that, for even though I liked Simon and wanted him to join me for my ongoing messes, I understood. His move was, if nothing else, mature.

"Should put your friends before yourself though . . ."

"Maybe, but not before your family or loved ones. Those must always come first."

"You know, it's quite hard to be angry with people when you're arguing for them."

"I do aim to please," I snarked.

"Still, try to not kill yourself training, would you?"

"I said I aimed to please, didn't I?"

He laughed and pulled a small bundle from his jacket, tossing it to me.

"Sandwich. If you're going to keep going like this, you'll need your energy. Things will be far worse if you're not in good shape to continue your training, won't they?"

"That," I said as I opened the little cloth package and took a bite, "is a very solid point."

I hadn't realized just how hungry I was until that first mouthful, and then my stomach went into overdrive. Within moments I'd scarfed the whole thing, not even leaving crumbs. Of course, I was well prepared for food issues. Having learned my lesson well from our first year, I kept a small stash of dried meat and fruit in one of my suitcases, enough for a snack or two, and long lasting so I didn't worry about replacing it too often. As I unloaded that bundle, Lucas laughed.

"Seems I didn't need to worry then, did I?"

"No, but I appreciate the thought. Want some?" I asked, offering a few slices of dehydrated apple to him.

"I'll pass."

"Your loss." I smiled at him. I'd had few friends like Lucas in my other life, and in some ways he was almost like a cousin or what I imagined a brother would be.

"What?"

"Just thinking about the past, my friend. Glad you were there with me."

"Bah, don't get all sappy on me; leave that for the girls," he said, reaching out to flick me on the forehead.

We laughed for an hour or two more, sharing jibes and barbs, along with a few jokes we'd both heard a hundred times. It was a good first day, but eventually I did kick him out so I could go wash and sleep.

Over the next week I stabilized. The training was still brutal, and I wasn't sure it was helping at all, but I got used to it. There was even time for me to do my schoolwork here and there, making sure my grades were maintained, for if they weren't, I was sure to hear about it from all sides.

CHAPTER 30

✶

SLOW STARTS

If I was making progress, I certainly wasn't seeing it. Every day seemed the same, with more tests, more meditations, and more shocks from that damnable rod of Sir Kendrick's. No matter how hard I tried or how long I practiced, I never seemed to be able to block out the attack completely, always feeling it race across my skin with each tap.

He did at least introduce some small changes in the exercise though. Some days I was given short exercises to do while he poked me here and there throughout—jumping jacks or push-ups—and other days I sat in various positions. Sometimes we moved throughout all these things in one day, but more often than not, we kept to one at a time.

I didn't complain, though, for I knew it to be a waste of time. They were determined that I learn this, and as soon as I figured out whatever problem I was having, I would excel. My instructor didn't seem bothered in the least bit by my lack of growth in resistance, pointing out when my attention lapsed but occasionally commending me on maintaining my resistance while working. There were other changes though.

"How are you doing today, Percival?" Sir Kendrick asked about halfway through a session.

"Well enough," I said. "Would you mind if I asked a question?"

"Of course not."

"I feel stronger, faster, my senses sharper, like they're all slowly growing," I said, and it was true.

"You remember the pushing and how it increased your abilities?" he asked.

"Yes, sir."

"It's that," he replied. "Your body is adapting to releasing more mana at once, strengthening you. This isn't your baseline, but rather this is you subconsciously using your power to empower yourself all the time. Do you understand?" he asked.

"But I don't feel like I'm doing that," I said.

"I'd have to get a caster to look you over, but at this point in the training almost everyone begins to release their mana as a reaction. In time you'll get more control, which will continue to increase your magical resistance; or, if you decide to learn the method, it'll help you hide your aura completely."

"Hide ... completely?"

"Yes, the same thing we're doing now just in reverse, but don't worry about that for the moment. These things come in time, Percival, and there's a reason we do them in a certain order. It makes the training easier. In years past, there were many methods, but those are gone now, replaced with modern techniques. These techniques work better, we are stronger for them, but they come in an order."

"Yes, sir," I said, nodding, knowing that arguing would be useless. He'd teach me when he was ready to teach me.

"Good. Now, I've arranged for a bit of a test of sorts, one week from today. Before that, though, we need to practice your actual fighting while using your resistance," he said.

"What sort of test?" I asked.

"If I told you, that would make the test less effective. Trust in the process."

"Yes, sir," I said tiredly.

"Good, now go grab a practice blade and we'll begin."

It turned out our new exercise was to spar while I kept the resistance going. It was a bit of a struggle, but there were some benefits. Sir Kendrick didn't really like to talk much while practicing, instead letting his weapon speak for him. He could hit me at will with the rod, but there were times when he used his own practice blade to slap me.

It didn't take me long to realize that each strike from the knight's wooden sword was to correct my stance or my attack, and I began to watch. I copied some of his own moves here and there, taking blows when I did them wrong, but picking up new tricks fast. It also fixed some issues in my own fighting style that I didn't even realize I had.

For days we continued, and I felt like I was actually learning something from him. Not resistance. No, that was still evading me; but instead, hand-to-hand combat from a master instructor who was devoting all of his time to me and me alone. It was something few got, and I wasn't going to waste it. This man was a personal servant of the king and for that reason had to be supremely skilled at his art, better than all my previous teachers, except perhaps the headmaster, and Headmaster Logan hadn't trained me like this.

Before I knew it, another week had passed. The days had slipped by me, between work and actually beginning to enjoy my training. This time, rather than our normal setup, Sir Kendrick met me in the arena, and he was not alone.

"Professor?" I asked, as I saw Professor Ruian had joined him.

"Hello, Percival," she said. "Doing well?"

"I am, ma'am, but why are you here?"

"The good professor will be helping with your test, Percival," Sir Kendrick answered for her. "You two will spar, with your goal being to touch her, and touch only—don't strike—with your practice weapon. Her goal will be to keep you from doing so."

I blinked a few times. The professor was, as far as I knew, a caster of some form, being that she taught magical item creation classes, but I hadn't imagined I'd be fighting her. I was also a bit nervous about actually trying to go against a teacher, something that normally wouldn't be tolerated, and even more so with a female teacher.

"Are you sure this is all right?" I demurred.

"Oh, don't worry, boy," Professor Ruian said, waving me off. "I've faced worse than you. And remember, you're not actually to hit me, just to try and touch."

"Places," Sir Kendrick said with a small smile, "for you may one day need to battle against women. Don't get hung up on it now."

As a point of fact, I'd had to fight girls, albeit of a goblin persuasion. Should this really be so different? With a nod I went to my side of the arena, taking my stance and getting ready.

"There will be three rounds. On my count, begin," he said before slowly counting down.

At zero I surged forward, and the professor threw forth her hand.

CHAPTER 31

★

TESTING MY RESISTANCE

I was a little anxious about fighting the little old lady that was Professor Ruian, but that changed in the first second of the battle. Around me the sands of the arena exploded in a wave, thrown back by whatever spell she'd hit them with. Even I felt the power slam into me, tossing me back a few feet like a hard wind in a storm. But I stood through the assault, blinking the dust out of my eyes as I tried to dodge any follow-up attacks. I could tell that even though I'd been affected, it wasn't as bad as it could have been. The circle we stood in was tossed away, but I'd only been thrown a bit. Seemed like I was making a bit of progress after all.

There was no time to bask in small victories, though, as the good professor seemed determined to give me a true test. As I was still recovering, several bright missiles flew forth from her hands, arcing wildly as they zeroed in on me. I began to bob and weave through the barrage of attacks, avoiding them with quick, evasive movements.

"You can't defend only the boy," Sir Kendrick yelled from the sideline. "Attack!" Sir Kendrick yelled from the sideline.

He was right, of course, and so without words, I dove toward my enemy, two of her arrows slamming into my side. They stung just a bit, but beyond that, there was no lasting change. That seemed to surprise her, and within a mere second I was beside her, lightly tapping her with the flat of the practice blade.

"Good show, Percival," she said with a smile. "Seems I'll have to try harder."

"Please don't feel the need, Professor," I replied, worried what would come next. As our next round began, she twirled her arms, and the small group of missiles she'd shot at me before looked like fireflies compared to the coming storm. This wasn't a handful of crows chasing a hawk but a full-on moving flock of starlings, buzzing like a swarm of angry bees.

"Shit," I managed as the wave crashed, moving toward me like a stampede.

Behind the swarm I saw the good professor releasing more and more of them, flowing from her hands and leaving trails in the air in fractal patterns. That gave me a hint, though, about the nature of these attacks.

Dancing around the edges of her still-growing attack, I tested my idea, focusing on protecting my hand and slapping one of the little attackers. It dissolved with almost no issue at all, feeling like a popping balloon against my hand.

Gritting my teeth, for I knew what I needed to do, I pushed my mana as hard as I could to the front of my body and charged, one arm up to cover my face. The result was loud, with the professor yelling in alarm as I passed through her cloud of defenders, each exploding like a tiny grenade against me but doing little. With a quick move, I touched her once again with the practice blade.

"Are you okay, boy?!" she asked, seemingly unconcerned about my win.

"Perfectly fine, Professor," I answered with a nod.

"What made you do that?" Sir Kendrick asked from the sidelines.

"With so many more coming at me, I knew they had to be weaker, and after testing my theory, the only way out seemed to be through," I told him.

The knight guffawed. "It worked, but don't depend on that in the future. It's a good way to get yourself killed against a more practiced opponent. Had she left most of her projectiles weak with only a few strong attacks mixed in, you'd have had a very bad time."

"Yes, sir."

Professor Ruian looked quite displeased now that she was sure I was fine, and I knew I was in for it now. It didn't matter how much I'd grown. She still had quite a few years of practice on me, and I knew the headmaster didn't have people on his staff who weren't good at what they did. Perhaps this wasn't her forte, but that didn't mean she didn't have something.

We reset once more, and she looked over at me, eyes narrowed. As our knight called us to begin again, there was no wave of missiles—no missiles as all. Instead, small glowing lines crisscrossed in front of me.

I tried to look for somewhere to dodge, but there was nowhere. The net closed in, and knowing that I couldn't avoid it, I once more charged, hoping to break the strands. That was a mistake. As soon as the first one touched me, it was like jumping into a spider's web. Quickly the strands grabbed on, wrapping me in layer upon layer of kinetic webbing.

My body was stuck fast, and I tried to push my resistance out. Slowly, the strands of my teacher's webbing began to slip off, dissolving or just finding no purchase on me. I nearly had a hand free as I saw her move again.

Sweat was pouring down Professor Ruian's face as she furrowed her brows in concentration. As she did so, all around me the sand began to move. That was bad, very bad.

Like flowing water, the sand around me climbed up my legs, forming thick layers before seeming to harden into rock. I struggled but couldn't break it off where I was tied up, and once it hardened I had no leverage at all. First one leg, then the second were submerged, and my hips followed not long after. She was nice when she got to my chest, leaving me plenty of room to breathe, even if I couldn't move much. Inch by inch she began to cover my arms, and I got desperate.

I tossed my sword, not hard, but hard enough to make it to her. Sadly, it missed, but it did make her flinch, ducking to the side and giving me a moment of respite. In that second I tried to break away from her trap, but it just wasn't enough. I was held fast in the layers of magic.

"That's enough, I think," Sir Kendrick said from the side.

"Very well," Professor Ruian said, releasing me, the stones cracking and falling away before finally returning to the ever-present sand.

"Remember, Percival, that resistance will only help against direct-spell effects. Summoned or controlled elements will bypass it completely, and need to be dealt with in other manners," he told me.

"Right, sir. I remember." He had told me that in the past, but I'd never actually experienced it. If water was summoned and controlled, my new ability wouldn't help me at all—the same as the sand the professor had used. Not everything could be stopped that way, and I needed to keep that in mind. "Do you mind if I sit for a moment?"

"No, I need to talk to the professor anyway," he said.

Though those spars had only lasted a few minutes, my body was shaking. Adrenaline and stress had built up in those moments, along with the full expenditure of effort, and I was spent. So, while they talked I went to sit on one of the stands, laying back and breathing deeply.

"I thought you were going to keep to direct attacks?" I heard Sir Kendrick whisper as he got close to his guest instructor.

"If I'd done that, the boy would've won every round. What in the world kind of training have you been giving him?" she returned in an equally low tone. They probably didn't realize that I could still hear them.

"Keep your voice down," he said. "Did you actually try?" he asked.

"Of course I did. I wasn't going to hold back to keep an ego intact."

I wanted to laugh. Here I'd been thinking that I wasn't making any progress at all, but it seemed my instructors disagreed. Of course I couldn't laugh, though, or I'd give away just how good my hearing was, and it was good to keep one or two cards close to your chest. Had this been a real battle, I'd have been in trouble, but had this been a real battle, I'd have shot the professor long before those spells got to me, so I was happy enough.

"Percival!" Sir Kendrick yelled from across the arena.

"Yes, sir!" I replied, sitting up and looking to him.

"Good work! You pass, if barely. I want to see you working harder though. Don't think just because you managed this that your training is anywhere near done."

"Understood," I said, nodding to him.

"Off with you; get some rest."

With another affirmative nod, I left, keen to get a bath while the baths were still empty. However, as I left, something struck me. Normally, if teachers wanted to have a private conversation, they'd use a small bubble spell to keep ears out, but they hadn't. Had they really forgotten, or had I been meant to hear their words? It sent a chill up my spine, for I knew that if I was meant to overhear them, and I slacked off even a little bit, failure would not be taken lightly.

CHAPTER 32

✶

GRATIFICATION

It was at least gratifying when Lucas began his resistance training. I'd had to go through mountains of it, but his first few days he was spent. I even got to reenact his little talk with me that first day I'd missed dinner.

"Are you going to be all right?" I asked him as he lay on his bed, seemingly unable to rise.

"Eventually, but everything hurts."

"Yes, I'm quite familiar with it," I pointed out.

"How did you get past this?"

"Same way you get past anything else—practice."

"Ugh."

"Sit up, I'll run you through a few exercises," I offered.

"Not going to poke me with some terrible stick are you?"

"No." I was at least pleased to hear that this seemed to be the standard method, not just something Sir Kendrick had cooked up for me.

From what I could gather, Lucas and the other fourth-year students were getting a similar, if less focused, regimen to what I'd gotten. They weren't really expected to get too far with it; after all, this was just an introduction for them. They also weren't spending nearly as much time in a day working against outside magic. Nor did I get the feeling they'd be keeping up this training as long as I was. No. Instead, it seemed like just another subject to teach the students and move on, like a single class and no more.

In the end they would lose out on fighting against magic, but that might be intentional. It wouldn't surprise me in the least if the government was keeping a lot of secrets from us, specializing their civilians in one direction that wouldn't be a threat to the military. In fact, since we were largely expected to be rich boys, and many of us weren't going to go to war, it made perfect sense. Teach us only the basics so that mages might be employed against us.

Surely there was training for the mages that was similar too. It wouldn't surprise me in the least if there were some gaping holes in the training that Rowena or any other number of wizards were getting, holes that would open them up should they ever rebel against the government. Briefly, I wondered what those were and where they'd left chinks in the armor.

It bothered me, but then I realized that my government back on Earth would have done the same. There's no way they'd have let people with superpowers run around with a full suite of training and no oversight. Heck, they'd probably have kept a very, very close eye on all of us, too, looking for anything dangerous.

"You're staring off into space again," Lucas pointed out.

"Hmm? Oh, right, as I was explaining you need to hold your mana and push it. The sensation is odd, but think of it almost like charging a magical device."

"I never really do that," he admitted.

"What? Really?"

"Yes, just doesn't come up often."

I was flabbergasted. That was a primary way for us to make money, and he just didn't do it? Maybe his parents were spoiling him, not making him get his own pocket money, but nearly everyone here did it.

"Well, that explains why you're having such a hard time with this. Don't you have an enchanted sword? How do you charge that?"

"What? Oh, I rarely ever use the enchantment on it. Even then, I've only had to charge it once or twice. And..."

"And?"

"And the servants at home do it while I'm there..."

"You're profoundly lazy, you know that?"

"Hey! I'm quite busy, and I get more than enough of that nonsense from my sister, thank you."

"If she's right, she's right."

He halfheartedly punched at me but seemed unwilling to rise. It brought to mind those first few days of training I'd gone through, and even if he wasn't going as hard at it, I understood that.

In time, I got him to stretch a bit and even meander off to go bathe. I also learned that he hadn't followed my good example and kept snacks in his room. That was painful to learn. He'd seen me do it, and even knew why I did it, but hadn't bothered to so much as grab some dried meat? Shameful, absolutely shameful.

Leaving him to his evening, I moved off, for I had work as well. Always more work, always more to do.

When I got back to my room, I looked at my mail and found a surprise. There were always letters from friends—Rowena and various parts of my family. Letters were huge, like phone calls or texts, and so I spent time every day dealing with them, responding and trying to be generally thoughtful. My parents, however, seldom sent me letters during the semester. Today that changed.

There among my normal papers was a thick envelope from my parents. Much of it was just them keeping me up to date. They'd been busy back home, it seemed, and while Mother hated the city, it also seemed they'd be coming here before too long. Mother had also included a huge packet of information about the burgeoning planes. It seemed Grandpa had been building a few more, and people were interested. Those people had, of course, gone to my parents, rather than my grandpa, who'd tell them to shove off, or rather than me, who'd do much the same. Poor fools had underestimated my mother, and a brief look told me she'd buried them under a deluge of paperwork, the backend of which I was now getting to see.

It all culminated with something that I'd not been expecting. She provided the dates that they'd be coming to the city, a couple weeks from now, and it seemed they'd be staying well through the next winter. It seemed she'd left out exactly why that was, but I'd find out when they got here, for there would be a reason. That much was clear.

CHAPTER 33

★

JOY AND TEARS

There was at least one advantage to my new schedule, and that was flexibility. Most of the time when we were at school, we were at school. However, with personal training being the bulk of what I was doing, I could finish up early in the afternoon before one of our off days and, well, go home. Perhaps in my first or second year I'd not have been allowed to do such a thing, but now . . . nobody seemed to mind.

And that was how I found myself heading back home one early afternoon. I'd only get to spend the night with my family. I'd not seen my parents in a year, and it would be nice to catch up. Perhaps we weren't that close, but I still cared for them.

As I strolled up to the door, I received an unexpected surprise—Mother coming out to greet me. Rather than send one of the maids or housekeepers to wait, she must have stayed at the door herself, looking for me to pull up to the curb.

The moment the door was closed she wrapped me in a tight hug. It wouldn't be proper for her to do so outside unless something insane had happened, but just inside the door she didn't hold back.

"Oh Percival, you've grown so much!" she gushed.

"Not really . . ." I demurred. Though, in retrospect, I had by about an inch or two.

"Nonsense, come in, we've got to catch up."

"I suppose you're going to tell me how displeased you are that I took the plane?" I asked as we sat down.

"I hadn't planned to, but if you're going to bring it up, it was dangerously irresponsible. Your grandpa seemed satisfied with the punishment he gave you though."

"You're being strangely nice . . ." I said.

"Well, before I got here your grandma and I had a long conversation about me leaving you to what would normally be my work." Ah, that explained it. Mother might not be one to cross, but Grandma was an outright monster when she wanted to be.

I chuckled. "Yes, please don't do that again."

"Worry not, your father and I are doing it this time around. I think he's going through the ledgers as we speak." I raised an eyebrow. She'd somehow managed to pawn some of it off on Dad? That was impressive, and it showed that while she never complained, she must have really hated doing the paperwork herself.

"Think we'll see him before dinner?" I asked.

"Percival, be nice. Your father is . . . Well, he likes his work, and it makes him happy to do it."

I had nothing personal against my dad, but I just didn't understand him at all. He avoided us most of the time, getting deep into his own work and research, or whatever he did. He was distant, not cold, but just so far away that I never really got to know him. My few attempts over the years had all ended in failure.

Mother had been formal for most of my life, but she was around, present and happy to spend time with me. If I went to her and tried to make some connection she seemed happy to have it, but my father, not so much. She and I, even though we were separated like men and women in our society were, still talked, still spent time together. She'd even given me some of my first training with the sword and never missed a tournament if she could help it.

Father still cared, I thought, in his own odd way, but it was like there was some blockage between us. He'd given me my sword, he'd spoken to me once or twice, and even appeared one time when I'd taken a bad loss in a fencing match to pat me on the back, but it was like he just didn't understand what to do at all.

Not sure what to do with the feelings I was having, I ended up sitting down and telling Mother about my schoolwork. I was leaving out a lot of the various attacks; she could hear about those from others. We even discussed my current relationship with Rowena, something she was more than eager to talk about, giving that whole part of our conversation her rapt attention.

Soon enough we'd worked our way through most of the events I wanted to talk about, and she got on to what they'd been doing. She and Father had spent last year doing a bit of light traveling through the kingdom, never too far from our summer home, but enough to get to places they'd never been before.

"Honestly, it was the best thing we've done in years," she concluded. "I know I'm expected to come here now and then, but I truly don't like this city. When you graduate I might never come back."

"Why?" I asked, surprised.

"It's stuffy, small, and smells devastatingly bad. More than that, frankly, I dislike the Season as a whole. Seems like a grand waste of time and effort."

"Yet you're here now," I pointed out.

"To see you. Your father and I talked about it, and though you'll eventually inherit all the estates, we thought you might like to stay in this house in a couple years when you graduate. It would give you some . . . privacy, particularly should you and Rowena decide to marry."

"Is . . . is that why you left me with all the paperwork?"

"Um," she nodded thoughtfully. "And I hate it."

That made me laugh. "I'll think about it, but don't rush things."

Time was limited, and soon enough it was time for dinner. I hadn't had dinner with them properly in so long, and though it was a bit formal for me, I still liked it. There was a little chatting with my father, who looked bothered for some reason, and dishes that I liked much more than those from the school.

When we were finished, we split for the evening. Since I had tomorrow off, I'd stay here. After all, my bed was much better than the one provided by the school. As I passed the servant's quarters I heard weeping and muffled voices from deep within. That was odd, very odd, so I listened for a moment more.

"Shh dear, it's going to be okay," my favorite cook cooed, trying to reassure someone. "You didn't do anything wrong, and everyone knows it. I'm sure you'll get a good reference; there's nothing at all to worry about."

The response was unintelligible through the tears that had to be flowing, but I knew the voice, the tone, the sounds. Without hesitation I knocked on the door to their quarters.

A few moments later Mrs. Rider opened the door a crack, looking out at me.

"Why is Kaylee crying?" I asked, trying to keep my voice steady.

"Sir, really, this isn't something you should get involved in," she answered, trying to close the door.

She tried but failed. I'd placed my hand upon it, and though Mrs. Rider might be strong in many ways, my body might as well have been an iron doorstop.

"Why is Kaylee crying?" I repeated, letting just a hint of the fury I felt creep in, and I saw her pale. Perhaps I wasn't known for anger, but she knew well just how dangerous I could be.

CHAPTER 34

✱

CONFRONTATION

"I will have an answer," I said, voice hard as steel and cold as ice.

"Sir, please calm down. Really, it's fine; everything is fine." Mrs. Rider had never seen me angry, truly angry, before. As a point of fact, few people had. Irritated, sure. Unhappy, all the time. Even a bit mad? Yes, that happened; but the cold fury working its way through my veins now was something rare.

"Then you can answer me."

"Your f-father was working his way through the finances and found we had too many maids, so he decided to . . ."

"Did he now?" I finished her explanation for myself, gathering clues from what I'd heard before. "And how many did he let go?"

"Just one sir. Kaylee is the newest and so . . ." She let the sentence die, and I understood.

"Have her return to her duties. I will speak to him of this." My piece said, I turned on my heel and began to walk away.

For years I'd thought about how I felt with Kaylee around but never really considered how my father felt. It must be such a *burden* for him, seeing the child he created but never took care of. That was the true reason for this—shame, shame and an unwillingness to do what was right. Well, if he couldn't be the man he needed to be on his own, I would have to take care of it myself.

I could hear my mother's calm breathing coming from her room as I passed, telling me she'd already gone to bed. Good, I didn't want her involved in this at all. My father had retreated to his office after dinner, as he so often did, obsessed with his work.

There was no stomping, no noise as I moved, slipping through the house like a silent thundercloud, promises of fury building as I made my way to his workroom. This was a place I had seen few times and had been allowed to tarry fewer. That hardly mattered now.

The door opened easily at my touch, and I closed it behind me. He sat there, leaning over several vials of one substance or another, a notebook open before him. He looked up, blinking in surprise and sitting back, eyes widening as he registered my expression.

"Percival, why are you here?"

"What exactly do you think you are doing?" I snarled.

"Whatever do you—"

"Kaylee," I said. "Do you think you can throw her away? Your daughter, my *sister*? What foolishness entered your thick head to lead you to that plan?"

"That's nonsense boy," he retorted, "and I am your father. You will address me with—"

"The respect by which you have comported yourself," I spat in response, teeth grinding. "Do you think me a fool who hadn't noticed? I knew before I could speak the words, as do Grandfather and Grandmother. No, I held my peace since I was assured she was safe, biding my time until I could do right by her, and you think I'll allow this?"

"You'll allow?" he said, bass seeping into his voice. "This is my home, and I will say what is allowed. I will see that there is propriety, and it is clear I must correct your behavior."

I felt the spell wrapping around me, something he'd cast, something quick, something to bind. With a flex of my will and an internal push, it shattered like paper-thin glass. My training proved its usefulness, and I was upon him. My sword, the one hidden within the cane that he himself had made for me, slid from its sheath and stopped an inch from his face.

"Propriety? How about I take my sister to our grandparents after carving her name into your forehead? What will your propriety say then? Oh, I imagine the rumors will be terrible, and Mother would want to know, too, wouldn't she? They offered, you know, when I was still small. Told her mother to come to them if they ever needed help. I'm sure they would take us in without a second thought."

He didn't try to cast again. There were rules in this world. Wizards and priests were terribly powerful, but once a physical magic user like myself got in melee range, it was over. No spell would stop me before I could slice him to ribbons, and we both knew it. One chance was all I'd needed.

"Son," he said, voice coming down, "calm yourself before you do something you'll regret."

"If I were not in control, you would not be able to speak," I said through gritted teeth. "So, what will it be?"

His eyes searched mine, then looked around for some way out, but there was none. I would make good on my threat, and he knew it, somewhere deep down. There was also some shame there, a tinge, like he understood on some level that what I was doing was what he should be doing to himself.

"Put the blade down, son. If . . ." he seemed he was going to say something but changed his mind. "The girl can stay."

With a swift movement I withdrew my blade, slipping it into the cane where it belonged. He sat back down, almost falling into his chair. I could see his hand tremble slightly, the shock of what had just happened still sinking in.

"I do not care if you speak to her, or acknowledge her, or anything else, but should you try anything like this again, I will take time out of my busy schedule to personally teach you how to unfuck yourself."

That might have been the first time he'd ever heard me curse, but he didn't acknowledge it. He simply continued sitting there. I turned, leaving him to, honestly, I didn't care.

The door was open, cracked, and as I approached, I heard the sound of heavy breathing, saw the small eye just behind it. I opened it and stepped out into the hallway, shielding Kaylee with my body from our father's view until I could pull the latch closed behind me. Her eyes were saucers, flicking between me and the door behind me.

"Come downstairs," I told her as gently as I could. "We'll talk. Everything is going to be okay." Poor girl must have had quite the day, and this was not the best way to learn this kind of thing. Though, would there be a better one? I didn't know.

"Your . . . my . . ." she stumbled.

"Yes, now let's go. I'd rather not have this conversation overheard. Don't worry, I'll take care of you."

She blinked again, and her eyes settled on me, on the small, pained smile I knew I wore. With that, she let me lead her down to my workshop, where we could finally talk as we should have long ago.

CHAPTER 35

✶

BETWEEN SIBLINGS

"Please, sit," I said to Kaylee as I closed and locked the door; no reason to risk someone else overhearing us.

"Um . . . sir, I really don't . . ." I gave her a look, and she sat.

Sitting in the presence of your employer was considered inconceivably rude for someone like a maid or member of staff. There were exceptions—jobs that needed to be done sitting down—but for the most part, they stood when we were around, a measure of respect, I think.

"You can also drop the polite speech, at least in here and for now. We may have to pretend for others, but now that you know the truth, there's no reason to when it's just the two of us."

"You've told me that we're related, but not how you know. How do I know this isn't just something . . . I don't know."

"People don't think little kids listen, but they do. I did, and my memory is sharper than you'd believe. Consider also how if I'd been wrong, our father would've simply told me such, rather than that embarrassment. If you're truly worried, we could have a priest check. That is well within the remit of their abilities."

She was still in shock, it seemed, still trying to process, taking her time. I let her. There really was no need to rush.

"So, I'm a noble?" she asked.

"No, not legally, at least. Barring an act from the king, even if you did get confirmation from a priest, without Father recognizing you officially, you'd be considered illegitimate. You could push for that, but if you do, I'll warn you that you'll be a pariah. Without that paperwork signed by him, I'm afraid that no well-to-do family would hire you; and while Grandmother and Grandfather Shadestone would surely take care of you, they won't be around forever."

"That seems terribly unfair," she said.

"It is," I agreed. "I'm sorry."

"Don't be, it's not your fault. Is there truly nothing you can do though?"

"I'm afraid not. He has to be the one to sign those papers. If your magic manifested fully, we might be able to put pressure on him, but unless it does." I ended with a simple shrug. That was all I could give her at the moment.

"I've heard there are medicines that can," she suggested.

"Then you've also heard that those drugs are fatal. Not once have I heard of anyone surviving long after taking them to increase their power. A few years at most before it burns your body out and you die. Personally, I'd appreciate it if you didn't take such measures."

"Perhaps it would have been better to not know," she mused.

"Perhaps, but now you do, and now at least I can make moves to help you that I couldn't before. Father might be worthless on this account, but I won't toss you aside, and one day I will be in charge of the family's estates. Until then, I can at least help you without having to make up reasons or excuses constantly."

"The items you gave us . . ." Good. She was smart, thinking about things.

". . . were really only for you. I made the others just to hide the fact that I wanted you to have a proper weapon and shield, should something happen when I wasn't around."

"Thank you," she said. "That was kind."

"You don't need to thank me. Taking care of you is my job." As I said it, I thought back to a fictional character who'd told a foolish man the very reason older brothers are born first.

She snorted, "I'm pretty sure taking care of you is *my* job, or it was."

"Still is. Father may be many things, but foolish enough to think I would make a threat rather than a promise isn't one of them. You don't need to go anywhere, and if anyone tries to make you, contact me and I'll handle them."

"Even the lady of the house?" she asked, referring to my mother.

"If I have to explain things to her, I will. She'll be furious, but not at you. May make things more complicated in the long run, though, so I'd rather not just yet."

"I see."

Plans upon plans began to form in my head, but as they did, I realized there was one question I hadn't asked.

"What do you want?"

"That's . . . I hadn't even considered it. I don't know." Kaylee looked at me, and I understood. She was still in the processing stage. She'd need time.

"You can stay as you are, working as you are, though with more backing from me. If I can get enough power both politically and financially, I might be able to force father to acknowledge you one day. That could be difficult, but possible." Even as I said it, I realized I knew several of the biggest players in the country, including the king, at least in passing. Those connections might one day serve to fix her situation, but that would be a major request.

"And then?"

"Well, you'd be able to stay either with us or with our grandparents as a full member of the family. It would be quite the adjustment, but it would be a good life."

"I understand. If I wanted that, what would I need to do?"

"The very best thing you could do would be to unlock your magic fully, and properly. There are no guarantees for doing so though."

"I don't suppose you have any advice on that?" she asked.

"Well, you use fire, right?" I asked, already knowing the answer. At her nod I continued. "Perhaps a greater understanding of how fire works and what it is would help."

I grabbed a small writing board from one of my drawers and began to scribble, not a normal commoner's understanding of fire from this world, but what I knew of it. Perhaps I'd not gone too deeply into chemistry on Earth, but what was well understood by high school students eclipsed some of the best theories this world commonly offered.

I told her how fire was a chemical reaction and explained oxidation as well as I could remember it, about basic atomic structure and how those reactions worked. Honestly, it was a bit of an information overload, but I simplified it as best I could. By the end her eyes were dry and slightly confused.

When we finished, we walked back toward the servants' quarters, a place I needed to pass on my way to my room anyway. She went in, and only a moment later Mrs. Rider came out, looking at me with an expression I'd not seen on her in several years. Clearly, she too had something to say.

CHAPTER 36

★

UNHAPPY HOUSEKEEPER

"Young lord, I've held my peace for a long time, but there are limits," Mrs. Rider began.

"Excuse me?" I asked, a bit taken aback by her tone. I'd been angry earlier, and she knew it and got out of my way. Now I was in a different mood, so she knew she could get away with saying whatever was bothering her.

"No, no I won't. For quite some time I've seen how you favor that girl, seen how you look at her when you think others aren't watching, but tonight is beyond what I can overlook, my lord. I cannot have you in . . . relations with one of the maids. If it got out, it would be a scandal, and I'm not beyond bringing this to your mother. Your father perhaps listened to you, but I've known her a long time, and I assure you, she'll agree with me on this."

I was honestly taken aback. That she'd noticed I favored Kaylee wasn't too much of a surprise. It wasn't like I was hiding it or anything, but that she thought that we were, well, doing what teenagers were wont to do was something else. I also had to stop myself from laughing, because that would have been truly inappropriate.

"Mrs. Rider, I believe you've misjudged the situation," I informed her as calmly as I could.

"Oh? And you didn't confront your father, causing him to inform me the girl would be fine to stay, before running off with that girl into your private room for nearly an hour? Do tell me that isn't what happened." I had to give it to her; from an outside perspective it was suspicious.

"You do know that her mother was my nursemaid and nanny, correct?" I asked.

"I . . . I hadn't really thought of it, but that doesn't mean . . ." she began.

"Or that through my childhood I spent much time with the girl?" That wasn't too true, as we'd been separated after a couple of years, but she didn't know that.

"Hm."

"Mrs. Rider, my interest in Kaylee isn't of the nature that you seem to believe. When we were young I viewed her, well, almost as a younger sister, nothing more. My anger stemmed from those feelings, not any infatuation. And, as for the time in my workroom, I was giving her advice on magic, so she could hopefully grow, should she encounter problems when I'm not around."

The best deceits were sprinkled with truth. I couldn't tell her that Kaylee really *was* my sister, but I could tell her that we'd been childhood friends and that I'd come to view her as such. The magic part was partially true as well, as I'd given her a fair bit of advice on combustion.

"Then you'll have no issue with me taking her to the Temple of Lovers tomorrow to have her examined?" she challenged in a whisper.

"None so long as she doesn't, but should I find that you harass her about it, I'll be quite cross."

Priests, as far as I knew, could detect a number of things, and if one wanted signs of sexual relations, it was possible. The Order of Lovers were experts in all kinds of magic related to such, and if anyone could, it was them. Mrs. Rider doing as she'd threatened would put that to bed once and for all, and allow her to douse anything the other staff were saying as well.

This sort of invasion of privacy would be unheard of on Earth, but here it was merely frowned upon. While it would be a scandal for a noblewoman to be asked such a thing, maids and their employers getting into bed together was, too, but the privacy of staff was basically zero. Without some knowledge of their superiors they weren't supposed to have relationships at all, though many did.

Added onto that Kaylee's age, younger even than me, and the suggestion was invasive, but not altogether unheard of. Mrs. Rider probably even counted as some form of guardian since Kaylee's mother was at the main estate.

"Then I shall," she declared.

"Take the cost from the house's funds, Mrs. Rider," I informed her before turning, "and keep in mind what I said about being cross."

Kaylee

This was horrid, and I wanted to crawl into a corner and die. Mrs. Rider had been absolutely up in arms last night, taking me off into her office for a full interrogation once she'd finished speaking to Lord— no, my brother. She seemed convinced beyond reason that I had been with him, an idea that made my very skin crawl, and had been quite clear about what she would do if I refused to join her on this little trip.

Her plan was to go to the lady of the house, consequences be dammed, and inform her of her suspicions. That alone would cause me to lose my job, and who knew what else would come of it when she came down upon me and most certainly my mother too. That was, unless I proved that I was innocent.

The housekeeper had even taken my uniform last night "to be laundered," which meant she was checking it, of course. Neither of us said it, but both of us knew. That, too, was such an invasion, I wondered if she'd dare if she knew the truth. Dreams of living like a noble flashed through my mind sometimes. Anyone would want that, wouldn't they? To not labor and struggle and break yourself to keep others comfortable? It seemed too good to be true.

It also made a sort of sense. Mother had never talked about my father, telling me only that she hated to think about it. She also had no magic of her own, so mine was seen as a blessing, but if I was the child of a mage, that would've almost been a given.

"Greetings and welcome," a priestess said as she approached us, looking at me. "Come to get the young miss a Lover's Mark?" a priestess asked as she approached us, looking at me. She couldn't have possibly been more wrong.

I turned crimson, feeling it fly up my cheeks. Those marks, as they were called, were magical tattoos, made to prevent pregnancy, pretty much the opposite of why I was here.

"No," Mrs. Rider answered. "You see there's been an . . . accusation about my ward here, and I'd like to settle it if possible."

The priestess gave me a long look before nodding. "Please come with me." When the housekeeper tried to follow she was motioned back. "Only her."

The robed woman was tall, half a head above me, and walked with purpose to a small, private room. I'd been to temples very few times and had seen priests for medical treatment fewer still.

"Thank you for keeping her from coming," I said as the door shut.

"It is standard practice, as are the questions I'll be asking you next. I should inform you that I won't lie, but I also won't force anything on you if you don't want it."

"Ah, thank you," I murmured.

"Have you been assaulted in any way? At your age that's a real concern, and if you have, tell me now and I'll help you."

"No," I spat out.

"If the man was older, that's an issue too."

"What? No, nothing like that."

She gave me a long look. "You can tell me; you're safe here."

"I really haven't—"

"Having problems with a boyfriend then?"

"I— What? No."

"Very well, if you're ready, I can examine you, assuming that's all right with you?"

"Well, if you don't, it'll cause big problems. Do you . . . need me to undress or anything?"

"What? No! Has someone been having you undress for healing?" She looked completely stunned by that question, and not pleased in the least.

"I-I've never been to a priest for healing before. There was a butler who could fix wounds, and I guess I never undressed for him. Otherwise, it's just been nurses for exams and minor illnesses."

"Oh, thank goodness. No, just hold still a moment."

There was a small flash of magic and a weird static across my body, causing me to jump just a bit.

"Well, I can say you've not been with anyone in a few days, at least," the priestess said.

"Ever," I corrected her, getting truly tired of this woman.

"I can't check for that, just for recent signs. Are you sure you don't want a Lover's Mark though? I can sense your mana and see you'd be able to charge it yourself, even if not by much."

"No, thank you." Getting one of those would undoubtedly send a certain housekeeper into a fit, and it wasn't like I was even interested in anyone.

"Very well, all done then. I'll tell your employer you're innocent."

As we left I had to try hard not to shake my head. It was so weird how flippant they were about such things, as if it wouldn't be an embarrassment at all. They were just out in the public about it. Well, private here, but still!

CHAPTER 37

✱

ARTHUR

Arthur Shadestone

I sat in my office, unable to even wish my son goodbye as he returned to that school of his, unable to face him. It wasn't fear, no, for I wasn't afraid of what he would do. That boy had known about my indiscretion and held his tongue for years, taking his time and doing what he thought was right.

No, it was shame. Shame for the things I'd done. I'd betrayed my wife, whom I loved without end, and while I doubted she understood it, that had been the reason for distancing myself over the years. Too afraid that the truth would make itself known, would come to the fore one day. The pain of that action had cost me so much, more than I'd realized at the time, lost in my own lust.

Worse still was the shame for my child, the one I couldn't even speak to. The girl was mine, but I'd never so much as spoken to her, never once embraced her, never one time comforted her or given her any of the proper love a father should. What a failure of a man I'd become, to not even take care of my own child properly.

Beyond even that was what I'd tried to do. In my mind I'd justified it at the time, thought about how she'd be fine, how I would see that she had a good recommendation, a chance for a good job. That was a lie though. Being fired was a black mark and I knew it. In all likelihood, she'd have struggled to find anything, and who knows where she might have ended up.

A spell and my room was sealed so that I could bend my head down over my desk and weep, weep as the fool and coward I'd become. For a time I remained there, bemoaning my own failures, regretting all the horrid choices that had led me here.

"What have I become that my own boy must show me what I should do?" I asked the world. "What a blessing that even with such a pathetic father he still turned out as he did."

Though I may have done wrong, my son didn't. Seeing what wrongs I'd done, he came here himself to discipline me, like he was the parent and I the lying child. I'd even tried to harm him, only to find he was stronger than me. He'd been ready in that moment, ready to do whatever he needed for his family. Whether I acknowledged her or not, she was his family.

I'd seen her just this morning, passing by the room she was working in. Never before had I seen her react, but this time she squeaked as if afraid of me and hid herself. My own daughter hid her face from me. She was right to. I'd her put in the clothes of a servant rather than the dresses of the nobility she deserved. I'd abused her more than I ever should have. I'd failed her too much. Why did I even imagine myself fit to call her my child?

There was only one path forward, only one way to start to redeem myself for this failure.

Blinking tears from my eyes, I pulled open the drawers of my desk. One by one, I pulled out utensils—pen, parchment, seal, wax, and an envelope. The act steadied my hands just enough to write.

And write I did. Words I'd thought about long ago, the proper formal declarations that were needed. Word after careful word, I wrote the letter I should have written years ago, and when I was finished,

I took my seal, charging it with my mana as much as I could, and stamped the bottom. My hands shook as I placed the document into the envelope and wrote my son's name upon it. Knowing this task had been completed and that there could be no going back, my breath hitched, as if I'd been running afraid.

It would only be a few days until he returned for the Season, and I would give it to him then. I'd give him this house then too. Lucille and I had already discussed it; a bit early would be fine. It would give Percival a place to be with his sister, should he so choose. When it all came to fruition, I would need to beg Kaylee's forgiveness, and that of my wife, but that much I could handle.

"As soon as you return, my son, just as soon as you return." I placed the letter upon the corner of my desk, never out of sight, never out of mind, for if I failed here, there might never be a way back.

CHAPTER 38

✦

DISTRACTIONS

"OOF!" I flew across the arena, skidding along the ground painfully.

This wasn't the first time I'd missed a strike today. In fact, there'd been several now. It was, however, the roughest one I'd taken, as it seemed Sir Kendrick was getting quite tired of correcting me.

"You're distracted again," he said with clear irritation on his face.

"Apologies, sir," I replied.

"Don't apologize, fix it. In battle, not paying proper attention will get you killed."

"Yes, sir."

"Again!"

For the next few minutes I was back on my game; then my mind wandered again. It was barely a moment later that I was thrown once more. He'd seen it, the very instant I lost my concentration and he'd hit me.

"I would appreciate it if you didn't waste my time. What is going on?" he asked.

"Family trouble," I told him, not wanting to elaborate.

"Luckily, they are not here to see this. Once more."

Once more was enough, and the unhappy knight put up a hand when I rose, showing me that we were done wasting time with this for now.

"I don't suppose you'll tell me why you can't keep your head in the game?" he asked.

"It's rather personal, sir."

And it was. All I could think about was what my father might do. He could retaliate now that I wasn't there, and he could do so with extreme moves. That seemed unlikely, but it wasn't impossible. I needed to be there, for Kaylee, keeping an eye on her.

"Well, if you're like that on a battlefield, you'll get yourself killed. How will that do for your 'family issues' boy?"

"Not good."

Sir Kendrick heaved a sigh. "Is this something you can solve if you went home now?"

"Honestly? I kind of doubt it." I wouldn't always be there regardless of what I did.

"So if your immediate presence doesn't help, is there a long-term step you can take to do so?"

I thought on that for a few moments. I ran through possibility after possibility and came up sort of blank. There was no real concrete thing I could do at this very moment.

"No, sir."

"Then you need to put this from your mind."

"That is far easier said than done."

He laughed. "Well, that's true enough, but every soldier has to do it." I blinked at him and he continued. "Do you think we don't worry about children, wives, parents? Everyone does, and there are good and bad ways to deal with that."

"Good and bad ways?"

"Certainly, you can try to ignore it, pretend it doesn't exist, and that works for some people, for a while. Some, it works for even for a long time, but personally, I don't think that's the best solution."

"Do you have a suggestion then?"

"The questions I asked you. I always ask if there's anything I can or need to do, and if the answer is no, then I just accept that it is. I can't change the weather, I can't fight an army, but there are things I can do, and doing what I can is what is important. Worrying about things I can't change doesn't help; it only makes things worse."

"What?"

"What if a beast comes to my home and ravages it? Well, that would be bad, terrible even, but can I take steps to prevent this? Certainly, and I have. Would more steps be helpful? Maybe, but they would stop me from doing other things that are more important. So, I must accept what is and what I can do nothing about."

"So you just want me to give up on things I can't do anything about?"

"Not give up, accept. Do you battle the rain or simply accept that it's happening? No, naturally you cannot change some things, and as for how you deal with it, that is something you need to figure out. However, today is wasted. Go and work yourself out, doing whatever helps you concentrate. I honestly don't care so long as you don't bring this nonsense back tomorrow."

"Yes, sir, thank you."

"Get out of my sight." He said it roughly, but with how he'd spoken and the things he'd told me, I could tell he meant me to consider, not just go away. I gathered up some papers and went to the school's machine shop. This world had a few advantages for me over my previous one. One, our school decidedly cared less about weapons than any on Earth probably had in decades. That made sense since we were all being trained in combat and most of the student body had ready access to arms of some form. They also didn't really know much about what my designs were because they were just that, new.

These facts allowed me to make the last few parts I needed for one of my longer-term personal projects. The majority of it was at home, so there would be no way to know if I got it all perfect until I returned, but I was really good at what I did, so adjustments would probably be minor. That was also why we had testing. Making ammunition and all the various bits and bobs I'd need for this had been something I'd had working for quite some time now, and by break it should be done.

As I worked, I fell into an almost meditative state, referencing and cross-referencing my measurements, holes drilled and pieces shaped. My hands worked, almost without effort, knowing these machines as I did. It wasn't mindless work, but it allowed me to consider, so consider I did.

Stressing wouldn't help my family, not one bit. On that Sir Kendrick was right. I couldn't change the way of the world right now, or force anything that I wanted to be true. I could, however, build my power, prepare, plan, and wait. I'd need more information, but my inventions were worthwhile, and what I was doing now was productive toward those ends. He was also very right in that if I didn't get my head in the game, I'd suffer for it and put everyone in more danger. I needed to trust, trust that those things I'd already done would function as well as they could, and trust in others to do what they needed to. That alone brought me some measure of peace.

CHAPTER 39

✶

WRONG

Sasha

The nest was always growing, always expanding, but I was getting worried. At first I hadn't noticed, but it seemed Father had been allowing some of our brothers and sisters to breed unchecked. Our hunters had been going out for big food hauls like usual, but I'd thought that had been mostly stored in case enemies attacked us.

It had not been stored, not at all. No, the newest generations were growing like weeds. Most of them were of the old kind, not special children like myself or Greta. There were also an alarming number who seemed to be spawned from my least favorite brother's loins, not something I'd been happy about.

Perhaps I'd ignored it, letting it slip my notice as I mostly dealt with the gate. Perhaps I'd not wanted to see it. However, in the last few months this generation had been hitting the age where they could start to go out into the world and explore. That had led to one after another stumbling over to where I was, and a brief look into the matter caused me more stress.

We needed to expand not only our population, but also our area for the nest. In some of the back caves there were goblins practically tripping over one another. They stayed back here, too, away from me, away from my smarter brothers and sisters. Father needed to know how far this had gone.

I slipped through the nest, aiming for his rooms, the ones he'd claimed to live and work in. Even if we weren't getting more subjects for him, he still worked, inspiring all of us to try just as hard as he was. It was good, too, for I always felt bad for the people he brought in. Even if they were helping make the world a better place, they still suffered and I hated that.

He was working when I found him, giving a demonstration to another like us who could heal broken bones and cut flesh. The youngling was just now learning to use his powers, but I'd sat through these, too, and knew that one day he'd be another asset to us. That alone brought a smile to my face.

"Does something bother you, daughter?" he asked once he'd finished and sent the youth away.

"Father, the tunnels are overflowing. We might need to help some of our people to . . . well, lower their birth rates. When I realized how many there were I came to tell you, but I should've seen it sooner."

"It is of no consequence," he responded.

"But, Father, where will we get the food for them? And the humans are still trying to find us. With this many it will be a struggle."

"Not for much longer," he said in a low voice.

"What?" I was confused, worried about what he was planning.

"Well, I was going to gather all you special children soon to tell you, but since you've done such a wonderful job there's no issue letting you know first. Soon we will go to the surface, and once we do, these things will no longer be a problem."

"I do not think the humans will like that at all," I pointed out.

"Probably not. We'll probably have to fight, but not to worry; I have a plan." That was good. Plans were good, but I still had concerns.

"They might want to fight us," I told him.

"They most certainly will want that, yes, which is why we need more of our own kind. Many more, in fact. That's why I've been encouraging the warren to grow for the last few years."

How had I not seen that? He was building an army, not just a new generation. My blood chilled at the thought of it, of how many would die if we fought.

"Their weapons..."

"Won't matter with enough of us. Most humans aren't very good at fighting, and once we've taken a few key points we'll be able to hold off those who are."

"But so many will die," I said, the worry in my own voice no longer masked.

"A sacrifice that must be made for a better world."

"... yes father, I understand."

I understood, but I didn't like it, not one bit. Years I'd stood guard over our home. Years I'd done all I could to protect us, to shield us. There'd been times when I'd worried about what he was doing, but I'd always known he wanted things better. This though; this disturbed me. He was going to throw so many of our people into battle, unprepared. And what if he was wrong? What if the humans were strong enough to take us, to hold the city? The young would die for nothing gained. And even if they didn't, how many of them would suffer? Too many.

It felt *wrong*.

The weight of that hit me like a club to the head, and my mana churned. We had to do right, those like Father and me, for if we didn't, if we did wrong, we suffered for it. I knew this, and so did he, and that's why I'd followed him, knowing he knew best. This was wrong though. It was so wrong, so very wrong. The word echoed in my head like a ringing bell, and my teeth clenched.

"Is something wrong, Sasha?" he asked. Yes, something was so, so *wrong*.

"I think I need to return to my duties," I told him, and I did—my duty to protect my people, the one he'd given me.

"Ah, very well. I'll talk to you again soon, my dear." With that I was dismissed, and I almost fled.

I had to go see someone, to talk to them, and I knew just the person. I'd go to Greta, the smartest of us, and we could talk this out, figure out how to make it right again. I found her easily enough in her little room hovering over some gadget.

"Sister, we need to talk," I told her.

Greta didn't always get me, but she always listened intently. I told her what our father was planning, at least what I'd heard, and of my worries. She didn't interrupt, didn't argue. She just waited, asking a question here or there, but letting me go on.

"What do you think?" I asked.

"They'll die in droves," she responded instantly, one hand going to her belly. She sounded shocked and worried. "Maybe we win, but we'll lose a lot. I looked at one of their new weapons, and they're not something to underestimate." I flashed my mana and saw the truth there within her belly. Maybe that was why she was so contemplative.

"So what do we do? Father doesn't change his mind once he makes it up."

"I don't know." That admission was enough to make me truly afraid for what might come."

CHAPTER 40

✶

END OF YEAR

Weeks passed without incident, turning into months. My infrequent breaks, sadly, didn't coincide with a good chance to return home. While I wasn't that far, Rowena was beginning to make noises, and through letters I could tell that Kaylee didn't need my immediate help.

My personal project, the one I'd been working on in my basement for nearly a full year, was finally finished as much as it could be without returning home to test something I was more than ready to do, but didn't have quite the time for.

As for my time as school, it all but finished, classes wrapping up and beginning their reviews before giving us exam after exam. On our final break day of the year, we all left tradition behind and studied rather than leaving or visiting loved ones. Third year was enough work for my fellows and myself to not have that luxury.

Before I knew it I was taking my exams, pen held between my fingers, scribbling answer after answer to my many teachers' questions. Even as I finished, I had to admit that I probably hadn't done as well as I would have had I kept going to their classes, but I felt I'd done well enough. There were little things I was missing, places from lectures I'd not seen biting me for not attending them, but it was okay. I still knew most of these subjects like the back of my hand.

Sir Kendrick had his own exam, as well, pitting me against several of my instructors one after another as he had before. This served a few purposes for him, I thought. Firstly, it gave me a good chance to see how a large number of casters would try to fight. He'd even managed to find a priest for me to go up against, something I didn't enjoy in the slightest. Second, it took me down several notches, for while I gave a good showing, I only barely won any of the matches. Finally, it let my teachers expend a bit of their ill will at my having been excused from their courses, and it was easy for me to tell who'd taken that decision personally. The math instructor in particular left me gasping for air on the ground after every match.

With all the examinations complete, we began packing, not that I hadn't prepared earlier. I was good and ready to get home, back to my family, back to the things I needed to do. Not everyone behaved the same way though. The last afternoon we were on campus I found Lucas sitting on the grass outside the school, staring wistfully at the various buildings.

"Something wrong there, brother?" I asked him, plopping down beside the senior.

"You know, for the last four years this place has been home to me. I think I'll miss it," he replied.

"What?"

"This was always where I returned, always where I came back to. It's home now, or close to it. Goodness, I only spent a few months at our winter mansion, and I've not seen the summer house since I started my studies. I wonder if my room there is still the same as I left it. Not that I can really remember all the details now."

I blinked for a few moments, then thought back to it, back to my life on Earth. While I'd not gone to college beyond some certificate classes, that must be what this felt like to him. This had been our home, our family. The headmaster had done everything he could to make it feel like our family, breaking us down to build us up, treating us like his little soldiers. It must be like leaving everything again.

"I . . . don't really know what to say to that."

"Do you not like it here?" he asked.

"Neither like nor dislike, but it isn't my home. So what do you plan to do now that you're done?"

"Hadn't really thought about it. I'll probably spend a couple of years with the family, running to tourneys and building up some money so I can get my own place. Then . . . maybe get married if I can find someone."

That sounds like a plan; maybe I'll do the same," I said, knowing that there was at least one knight who'd want me to continue my training.

"Pfft, at least I know where you'll be. Might hang around the city next year to keep an eye on you. Can't have you doing anything untoward with my sister, now can I? You two need a proper chaperone for your little study dates."

"I'll miss having you around here," I told him. I had few friends.

"You, too, Percival, you too."

For a time we sat in companionable silence, but all things had to come to an end, and so before I knew it, we made our way inside, putting the last of our things away and readying for the morning.

With the sun came the carriages, one after another taking us home. Some celebrated, particularly among the seniors, some seemed a bit relieved, quietly tired, and others seemed wistful. Lucas put on a strong face, ribbing and laughing with us, though deep down I could tell he still felt a bit conflicted. We'd known each other long enough. The small glances at the school, the sideways smiles now and then, but he was ready.

My own ride was one of the last, running a bit late for some reason. As I watched the carriage arrive at the front of the line, there were only me and a few younger students left. A porter came to grab my bags, but as he did I felt someone behind me and turned.

"Keep practicing over the break, Percival. I'll have a whole new setup for you next year," Sir Kendrick said with a laugh. "Maybe work on your observational abilities."

"Thank you, sir," I said, trying not to frown.

"Off with you, lad, and enjoy the break."

I made it home as the afternoon sun hung high.

"Welcome home, son," Mother said as I walked through the door. "Do you want some lunch?" mother asked as I came in.

"In just a bit. First I need to put my things away," I told her, motioning to the stack of luggage.

"Very well, but do try not to take too long. Your father said he wants to speak to you this afternoon."

That was a bit surprising, since our last conversation had ended with my blade inches from his face. After a few seconds of thought I nodded, preparing myself for whatever he had to say before heading to my workshop to deliver my newest additions to their places.

My bags of clothes could wait. This I wanted done first. So I slipped rods and pins into place, assembling parts that I'd kept in different drawers, lest my mother stumble upon this creation while being nosy. The weapon slipped together like it had always been perfect, the bolt sliding into place with a satisfying *clunk*.

The beast weighted almost a hundred pounds without any ammunition in it, and stretched across one of my larger benches. Three boxes of the needed shells were waiting, prepared in their links for testing as soon as I could get somewhere to do it.

"Look at you, beautiful. I always wanted one of these," I murmured to it.

I heard the door to the workshop and saw a smiling Kaylee in the doorway.

"It is good to see you, my lord," she greeted me politely, careful in case someone else heard her. "Your mother asks when you'll be joining—"

The room shook as an explosion rocked the house. I made it to her and caught her before she could fall, but as the sound of the blast faded, I began to hear screams.

"What was that?" Kaylee asked, her ears not as sensitive to the panicked people as my own.

"Nothing good," I responded, feeling a bead of sweat roll down my neck.

CHAPTER 41

★

INVASION

I held Kaylee for just a moment as the first screams of panic reached me, then I looked her dead on and spoke.

"Stay here, something is wrong."

She made a move to grab onto me, to keep me from going, but I was far faster than her, and in a moment I was out the door. Nothing in our house was burning or wrecked, so whatever happened must have done so outside. I wasn't the only one to think this, either, as our housekeeper Mrs. Rider had somehow made it outside already and was looking out in terror on the stoop.

"What's happening?" I asked as I rushed out to join her.

The screams were audible to both of us now, echoing through the streets as people panicked. There was a billowing cloud of smoke coming from nearby. Knowing for sure would be nigh impossible, but it looked like it was coming from the direction of the local guardhouse. Then I saw something that truly made my hair stand up. A city guard was being harried down the street by three goblins with simple clubs. The man had no weapon to be seen, fighting them with only his fists. Had these creatures been what I was used to dealing with—smarter, bigger, stronger—then he'd have been quickly overtaken, but these were smaller creatures, about child-sized, and he was putting up a good fight.

I flew to his aid like a loosed arrow, as he fended off the beasts the best he could. As one grabbed his arm, beginning to pull him down, I reached his side, the cane I carried freeing the blade as I joined the fray, the conclusion forgone.

"Quickly, we need to evacuate the people," I yelled at the man as I flicked my blade, trying to get some of the gore off of it.

"There are more coming," he replied, pointing to several more of the beasts making their way around corners and onto a nearby street.

"I'll hold them. Warn the people to evacuate." He looked at me as if I was insulting him for a second—doing his job for him—then thought better of it.

"Thank you, sir, I will."

As he ran to the nearest home, I turned to Mrs. Rider, still frozen on the stairs. "Quickly, get everyone out, now!" I yelled at her, causing her to quickly nod and retreat into the house. The next few minutes were chaos. Dozens of goblins made their way toward us, and I flitted around the street, cutting them down where I could, as I struggled to keep them away from the innocents. Behind me I could hear people running about, the sounds of horses and carriages being prepped, but there were so many goblins that I didn't want to look back.

It was then that the first variant came to join the fray, neither as big nor as strong-looking as the goblin I'd fought to save that little girl, but he towered over his fellows nonetheless. With a smile he charged, only to be met by a bolt of lightning from behind me.

"Can't let you show me up, now can I?" a gruff voice said.

One of our neighbors, an older gentleman with a thick mustache, strode down the street, arcs of energy dancing around him. Other residents were also slowly coming out of their homes to join me in the street. A man or two here or there was coming our way, looking thoroughly displeased at what had come to their neighborhood.

These weren't staff either. Not butlers or maids, neither footmen nor drivers, but the owners of these homes. Most of the men would be away during the daytime, but those that were here came to defend their homes, the powerful stepping forward while their people fled. Behind them were the ladies of the houses, organizing to get people out as quickly as they could with their own magic or strength. My mother was there, nearly throwing the cooks and maids onto the cart that had been pulled out front by our staff.

My family's safe evacuation confirmed, I turned back to the battle at hand. There were dozens and dozens of the goblins coming now, with a few odd ones sprinkled in among them. The plain ones were no issue at all, but the six or so who could throw small spells at us, or were speedy enough that I needed to deal with them, were an issue.

If there were dozens here, there had to be hundreds or thousands throughout the city. Those numbers chilled my bones, for I'd only ever seen a few goblins before now. How had they grown in number without us noticing? How many were there, truly? I didn't know, but it was clear we needed a much more potent response.

A few minutes more, and a shimmering barrier lit across the opening to the street. Behind me, I could see my father approaching, magic flowing around him as he reinforced the wall. He was tucking some papers into his jacket, a bandoleer of potions strung over his shoulder. Well, better late than not at all.

"That will hold for a few minutes. It's time to go," he informed the gathered fighters.

We ran for the cart full of our people, just as Mother helped Mrs. Rider in.

"That everyone?" she asked.

"Yes, ma'am," Mrs. Rider assured her as Father and I jumped on. "I checked the back rooms and quarters myself." Mrs. Rider assured as father and I jumped on after the two of them.

"Then we best be off," my mother called to the driver, trying to keep the panic from her voice.

We sped off as fast as we could, houses passing behind us, streets falling backward. I looked at the terrified staff, huddled into the small space, and took a breath. It was fine, it was going to be fine. Something was wrong though. Among the scared faces, one was missing.

"Kaylee? Where's Kaylee?" I asked, loud enough for all to hear. There was no response.

Then it hit me. I'd told her to stay in my workshop. My workroom was in the basement, and while I could hear through the ceiling and walls, someone without my senses certainly wouldn't be able to. The measures I'd taken to keep noise from bothering others would keep her from hearing the calls to evacuate. Why would anyone check there either? Mrs. Rider had seen me run outside, and all the staff had seen me fighting as they prepared to flee. She was still there, still in my workroom, as those goblins bore down on our homes.

For a moment my whole body went numb, the pain of what I'd done lancing through me. That lasted only a brief second before resolve hit. I clenched my jaw and the sword in my hand before turning and leaping from the cart. I heard gasps and a yell from behind me as I rocketed back the way we'd come.

Could I leave her there? No. I'd carve my way through every dammed goblin in this city to protect her and not think twice about it.

CHAPTER 42

✶

THE FORGOTTEN MAID

Kaylee

I waited in the odd, machine-filled room. Something must have gone truly wrong for Lord Percival to have run off like that. After the explosion, it had gotten real quiet. Not that you could hear anything down here, but the silence was a bit grating. Really, I could just peek upstairs . . . but he must have thought there was danger, and he had kept me as safe as he could.

Lord Percival. It was so odd thinking of him as anything else, even now. For years he'd been my employer, a bit odd, certainly favoring me over others. Before that an occasional playmate as little kids, but I could hardly remember it. Just Mother's complaints the few times he'd been around, but he was kind and gentle, and always seemed so far away.

He didn't think of me like that, though, did he? He'd known. He must have known for some time that we were kin. That was why he was like that with me. The little wand and shield he'd given to all of us were too much for servants—valuable magical items worth quite a bit of money. He'd made them because of me, though, because he wanted me safe. Was it wrong that I still saw him as anything but a brother?

Still unsure, I meandered about the shop, careful not to touch anything. He didn't like it when anyone touched his stuff, even me; though honestly, I doubted he'd be that mad. If I did touch something, though, it would still be really rude. After a few moments of wandering through the place I came back to the table he'd been at, looking at the gun he'd made.

For it certainly was a gun, though a very odd looking one. I was no expert on the matter, but this was a weird looking piece, with a massive barrel and odd, blocky center. There was some kind of trigger at the back, and a hole right through the center of what had to be the main chamber. That was odd, wasn't it? Did people make guns like this? Maybe something new he'd cooked up; he had made a few different guns after all. Beside it there was a massive box full of bullets, weird ones with a copper back and some lead- or steel-looking front, all bound together by a chain of some kind. They were almost pretty, if I didn't know how dangerous something like this was meant to be. Percival was a bit odd. He had physical strength in spades, so why would he want something like this?

With a sound almost like an explosion, the door to the room splintered to bits. I stood bravely, not ducking and screaming as my half-brother flew inside, covered in blood and sword in hand. He landed, looking winded, eyes flashing all over the room.

"We need to go now," he said firmly. Not yelling, but clearly making it an order.

"Go where?" I asked from under the table.

"The duke's castle, and quickly."

"What about everyone else?" I asked. There were lots of people in the house.

He winced and had a guilty look on his face.

"They already evacuated," he said. "When I realized you weren't with them, I came back. Hurry now."

After a quick look back he grabbed the gun, hurriedly putting the chain into the hole in the center. There was a clever little hinge there I'd not seen that thunked into place, and the box fit on the side. He even had a strap rigged to go over his shoulder to carry the massive contraption.

"Is that really necessary?" I asked.

By way of answering he took cotton balls and shoved them in our ears. "Are your items charged?"

"Yes, do we need them?" Panic began to creep up my spine when I saw his serious expression.

"I certainly hope not." He slipped the sword back into its sheath, and before I could start walking, he picked me up.

"What are you doing?!" I shouted as he began speeding through the house, not so fast that I couldn't see, but much faster than I could walk.

In a few seconds I saw the reason for his concern. There were bodies in the house, two of them, weird looking green men. I knew he'd fought goblins, but I'd not seen them before. These must be them, strewn about the rooms.

For a moment I bemoaned how hard it would be to get the blood out of the carpets and floors, and then caught myself. If there were monsters in the house, that meant everyone in this entire area was in danger. How bad was this?

My answer came only moments later when we got to the street. Dozens of the beasts were lying dead, cut, burned, ripped apart. There must have been a full-scale battle here I'd missed, sitting quietly in his workroom. What could I have done here? What if he hadn't come back? My blood ran cold at the very thought; but the warm arms wrapped around me reminded me that he had, that I had a defender, unafraid even to fight our father. A tear slowly made its way down my cheek.

As my heart thrummed, my brother seemed to almost glow. It was like little bubbles of light began to form across his skin, and then floated off. The sight was beautiful, like something from a painting. As he ran for the end of the street, carrying me in his arms, they floated down the road behind us.

Then he stopped.

"What's wrong?" I asked as we skidded, quite literally, to a stop.

It didn't take long for me to see and hear it. Down the road ahead of us spilled easily a dozen of the little green beasts, and a quick look behind us confirmed more were coming. They seemed different though. These were a bit bigger, a bit brighter in the light, and far more muscular.

"Not good," he said, as he sat me down.

"Do you have a plan?" I asked loudly, bringing up my wand and moving the bracelet to shield myself.

"I do."

"What are you going to do then?"

"Make Mr. Browning proud," he answered, pulling a lever on the side of his weird gun and letting it go. A weird *ca-chunk* echoed from it.

Who in the world was Mr. Browning?

CHAPTER 43

✱

THE MAN I SHOULD'VE BEEN

I'd never managed to own an M2 back in my previous life, but the Ma Deuce was legend. A weapon that had served in war for nearly a century. This weapon wasn't exactly that gun—sizes between worlds were certainly a bit different, and I couldn't remember the design exactly—but it was damn close.

With a heave I brought the machine gun to my side, the strap tightened, the sights . . . well not usable from this angle, but at this range it wouldn't matter. I thought back to the poster I'd had mounted on my old workshop wall, the one demonstrating how this worked, and smiled. This world didn't yet have the laws to deal with what I was bringing to the table.

"Cover your ears" was the only warning Kaylee got before I squeezed the slightly altered trigger.

The first burst erupted from the barrel in fire and thunder and shredded a small group of the approaching goblins. The gore hadn't even touched the ground before I adjusted my stance, aimed again, and fired. Short bursts, aimed at one group then the next, blasts of death, one after another. I needed to conserve ammunition, I only had a limited number of rounds.

At first my aim was imperfect, but soon I got the feel for it, with few shots going wide. Without the power magic had infused in my body, this would probably be impossible. The power of the round and weight of the gun rendered this operation inefficient at best and inconceivable at worst. My power absorbed the kick from the weapon, allowing me to keep it on target, letting me process faster than any man of Earth could and empowering me to shift my aim smoothly and accurately in ways I'd only dreamed of in my previous life. Even without the benefit of long practice, this was possible. I could do it. I could win. One side cleared. Enemies dead, dying, or fleeing, and then I swung around, facing the other direction. They seemed to sense their incoming doom, and the goblins backed off, diving behind pieces of broken masonry or carts, hoping for some cover from the death I'd brought. It wouldn't be enough.

More bursts, more light clinks as brass scattered across the ground at my feet. Behind me my sister was curled up close to the ground, hands over her head. Even with the earplugs I'd given her, this was still insanely loud. Another group of enemies became red stains.

Click

It only took a single look down to get it. The box of ammunition, the only one I had, was empty. Frankly, I couldn't have hoped for much better. This weapon and the ammo hadn't even been tested, and while I could now call it quite tested, that was all I had.

With a flip I pulled off the strap I'd used to hold the weapon up, letting it clatter to the concrete, the slightly glowing barrel clattering against the paved stones.

I let my eyes flip from the far side back toward the duke's castle. There were still a few goblins hiding, but most were dead. Now was the time to go, though, so I turned to my sister. Before I could scoop her back up, though, I saw another enemy enter the arena.

The goblin that came for us now was easily twice the size of the others, covered in rippling muscle, and familiar. He smiled when he saw me, the one I'd fought in the sewers, who'd tried to take that girl. This was the same goblin who'd trounced Lucas those few years ago.

He'd even brought friends. Behind what I could easily call their leader were his two companions, smaller than the first, but still a head taller than their other, lesser kin. All three were covered in gore, as it seemed they, too, had been having a time of it.

"Well, well, I wondered who was causing so much noise. You know, when Father sent me to lay waste to this place I was so excited, but had I known I'd see you again, I would have thanked him even more."

"Why? Why are you doing this?" I asked, hoping to get some information while I reached for my waistband and the pistol I had there.

"Hmm? Oh, Father wants something, something that he thinks will ensure our spread forever across these lands. Honestly, I don't really understand, but he told me there's a new place where we can build a nest, somewhere we'll be impossible to be dug out from. Doesn't that sound nice? That's not my job though. My job is to do as much damage as I can, make the soldiers come here to fight me, like you."

I drew, and before he could make it to me, I began to fire. The first was at his head, which he ducked, the bullet missing by inches. Then came his two helpers, one at each of us. Perhaps I could take him down if I shot with everything I had, but maybe not, and I couldn't fight three at once. My second shot went into the eye of his first lieutenant, coming out the back of his head in a spray of gore. The third clipped the other attacker, ripping through his shoulder muscles.

Then they were upon me. Two verses one, and they fought like rabid dogs. The big one had an ax he slashed and chopped with, trying to take me apart, while his companion used only his fists, his weapon lost when his shoulder became unusable. One crossing, then another, with all of us ducking and weaving. He'd improved, but so had I, leaving both of them covered in cuts even as my clothes ripped from the struggle.

Just as I lined up a stab to finish the larger of the two, the smaller goblin leapt forward, grabbing my arm and twisting. There was a popping sound, and I screamed, feeling the moment the bone was pulled from the socket.

It was enough to turn the tide, and they were upon me. I fought with my one good arm and my feet, but against two it was futile. Blow after blow fell upon my face, and my nose shattered, a spray of blood dripping down everywhere. I was out of tricks, out of things to try as they rained punches upon me. A hand wrapped around my neck squeezing.

"Good, good fight. When I'm done with you, I'll—" he said as my vision began to fade, the black edges creeping in. I needed to scream to Kaylee, tell her to run. If she left now, maybe she'd have a chance to escape.

"GET OFF OF HIM, YOU MONSTER!" The shrill scream was accompanied by a blast of light and heat, followed by the sound of broken glass.

I gulped air in as she stood, the wand I'd given her in hand and trailing just a bit of flame. The smaller goblin was singed, but they weren't gone. They charged at my sister before I could act. She brought her hand up, the bracelet forming a shield before her that stopped him dead, if only for a moment.

Then, with a flick of her wrist, Kaylee formed the trailing fire from the wand into a whip, wrapping it around the stunned goblin's neck. With a feral scream, she pulled, her flaming lash sawing through its neck like a hot knife through butter and sending the beast's head tumbling to the ground.

I blinked. That was not at all what that wand was supposed to do. For a moment my brain malfunctioned, trying to figure out how she'd managed to do what she'd just done. Then I watched her stumble, all strength seeming to leave her body.

"Kaylee!" I rushed forward to catch her, her eyes unfocused.

"Are you okay?" she asked, looking worried.

"I'll be fine."

"No, you will not," came a furious voice. The goblin she'd sent flying pulled himself through a house's broken window, bits of glass and shards of brick falling away.

His scowl was deep as he walked toward us, and then he was gone. A blue flash struck him like a freight train, sending him flying down the road, and walls of shimmering force sprang to life around us, harder, stronger than any I'd ever seen. I could feel the tingle of magic on my skin and looked toward the castle.

My father strode down the road, his bandoleer of potions quickly emptying as he chugged one after another. His eyes were cold as steel and full of hate, and he was literally glowing with magic. Across what skin I could see, pulsing blue veins began to spread. He grabbed another vial, emptying it into his mouth before tossing it over his shoulder, like it was nothing. In his wake was only destruction.

"Father?" I asked, looking at him as if he were someone I didn't know.

"That beast isn't dead; damn durable," he said.

"I've got her," I said. "We just need to—" I'd thought I couldn't be surprised any more than I already had, but I was wrong. He pulled Kaylee and I into a hug.

"Kaylee, my daughter, I'm so sorry for everything. I hope one day you'll forgive me," he said to her, "but for now you need to get to safety." Then he turned to me, pulling a letter from his breast pocket and shoving it into mine. "Percival, take your sister and go. Give that to His Grace. He'll know what to do. Go now! The way is clear."

My sword floated up, pulled back into the cane, and shoved itself into my belt. The pistol I'd had doing much the same as he split from us. The magic was so clear, so pure, arcs of power leaping off of him invisibly.

"Father?" Kaylee asked, looking worried.

He kissed her on the forehead and helped her into my arms, a difficult carry with a dislocated one, but possible.

"Time to go, dear. Trust your brother."

"If you can keep the way clear as we move—" I began.

"No, I need to clean up this mess." As he spoke, I could see the goblins regaining their fury, pounding on the walls he'd put up. "I'll be right behind you."

I recognized the lie for what it was as he pulled another potion out and drank it, the last one he had. I also saw the tightening of his jaw, as pain wracked him. Whatever those were they were hurting him badly, and he needed a priest now. Still, I couldn't stop him. As he smiled at us gently, I began to run, a blast of power clearing all visible enemies from my path as I did.

"Time to be the man I should've been before," I heard on the wind. It was barely a whisper as I leapt, bouncing up walls and buildings.

CHAPTER 44

ARTHUR'S END

Arthur Shadestone

As my boy carried away the daughter I'd never known, I watched, pushing back the tears. What was done was done, and it was time for me to go, to finish this. Steeling my resolve, I began to cast like never before.

The magic was so easy right now, coming to me in waves of power, moving to my will like instruments in a concert. With a wave I sent forth hundreds of missiles, slaughtering every one of the goblins nearest me. They didn't get one or two, but several each, enough to make sure there was no getting away. I heard a roar from a ruined building and saw—almost like feeling it through the magic itself—several lights from around the city speed my way. Excellent! Call all your best. I wanted them here to deal with me and not harm my children, not threaten anyone else. Yes, that was the play. Now I just needed to wait until they arrived.

My potions were gone, the best I'd been able to make consumed for just this battle. Each was capable of boosting a mage by a small amount, but at a cost. One potion when drunk would make you stronger for a time, but the backlash would likely affect your health for a few months. Two would shorten your lifespan by years; three, decades; and four ... Well, if you drank four and were tended to by a priest immediately, you'd perhaps live a year. I'd had eight, and even if the heads of every Order were here right now to tend to me, I'd still be dead by sundown.

That was fine though. I was a poor wizard at the best of times, easily eclipsed by my wife and son. However, I was smart enough to realize what was needed to kill the beast that had been attacking my son, and to clear the way for his escape. It would've been the death of me either way. Really, it was better to die quickly than suffer anyhow, so there was no need for regrets.

A series of attacks against my shield stirred me from my thoughts. The monster wasn't fleeing, but rather hiding and launching bricks, bits of pie, or whatever else it could find from the shadows before retreating. Normally, that would be effective. I wasn't fast enough to keep up with it.

It wasn't a battle of one versus a static opponent though; he'd forgotten that. The enemy always had a say, and if his say was that he wanted to play that game, I'd play one of my own. Stretching my hands out, I began to weave a net around us, around this whole block. From the outside it would be nearly invisible, but inside you'd be able to see the blockages. This was designed to let things in, not out. All of them closer to me, closer to their deaths.

More bricks and metal bobs hit my shield wall, pinging loudly.

"Going to keep doing that all day or come out?" I asked quietly. A few cracks formed as I drew the shield in.

"Going to kill you, then the boy, or maybe the girl first, let him watch. That would be fun, wouldn't it?" he teased, hoping to get a rise out of me.

"Don't think you'll manage that," I replied, shooting out a barrage that leveled the building he'd been in. More noise, more of a call to the others he was summoning.

"You're powerful, to be sure, but you can't keep it up forever; there are already weaknesses showing."

I smiled as I drew the shield in again, spiderwebs crawled across the surface. I saw more goblins pouring into the area; the fastest had already arrived. Good, just a bit longer to catch the casters who were slower to join the fight. I pushed more into the shield, letting it absorb more and more attacks. It seemed the one I was fighting was a leader of sorts, and with barked orders got the others to join in his barrage. I unfocused my eyes, seeing the strands of my aura, burning, consuming themselves faster and faster as the elixirs I'd consumed ripped their way through my body, magic igniting it like a pyre.

Beside me sat my son's newest weapon, some magnificent contraption that spat bullets like falling raindrops. That brought a smile to my face. What else could a father ask for than to be eclipsed by his offspring? There was nothing better than seeing my boy succeed in ways I'd only ever dreamed. How proud he made me, a shame I couldn't tell him that now. The casters finally arrived, seven or so coming into my net and launching attack after attack at me. Most of it was fire or pure force, simple spells. There was one using water though. Rather clever of him to use an element so commonly good against us.

As the attacks kept coming, the cracks continued to spread, turning my shield into something that more resembled bits of broken glass held together at the edges and slowly heating up. The fire burning through my magic leapt into them, causing the spell to ignite, but that was perfect.

The leader, the one I'd come here to engage, charged, a lamppost in hand, and began to pound on my shield.

"Not so tough now, are you? Not so strong! Soon this will break and I'll crush you like a bug!"

I laughed, a flaming tentacle of magic reaching out to wrap around him.

"What?!" he bellowed.

"Can't have you getting away. No, none of you can get away."

"You'll die here!" he spat, mouth foaming.

"That was always the plan."

I pushed the ignition of my magic to its peak, needing the boost of power. It would only last seconds before doing me in, but seconds was all I needed. The web tightened, and as I reached my hands out to pull, it heaved. Buildings were freed from their foundations and sucked inward, right to me, as I kept pouring power into the shield.

As everything around me was pulled in, I set my protection to explode, the pieces that had been shattering, hardening into a tiny sliver of blasting power, all shooting outward, all blowing apart as my mana did the same within me. With a smile on my face, the last thing I saw was the goblin's eyes going wide in panic and fear.

CHAPTER 45

★

TURNCOATS

I moved along the rooftops, something normally quite frowned upon. There were many people who could've done it, but running along the tops of people's homes didn't make you many friends. However, it was an emergency, so rules were quite a bit looser.

We remained still in the quiet for a few moments, letting the goblins slip past before Kaylee spoke.

"Is he going to be okay?" she asked innocently, hope filling her eyes.

"I—" There was a roar of fury that echoed behind us.

Before I could come up with an answer, I saw them joining us up here, several rooftops ahead of us and in our path. I instantly recognized the goggles, and the same outfit the other one also wore. The two goblin girls I'd met so long ago had shown up.

"I need to put you down," I informed my sister. "We've got company."

"No."

"What?"

"No," she repeated. "Whatever it is, we'll go together. You're not leaving me behind again."

I thought about fighting her as she tightened her arms around my neck. It would be simple to pry her off, but could I? Could I put her to the side and tell her to run while I knew I was going to a fight I couldn't possibly win? No, that was impossible.

"Fine, but follow my orders. These two don't play games."

I hated doing this, but I could see the goblin girls had already spotted me, their eyes locked on me. Neither had attacked yet, though, so perhaps there was some hope of them at least letting my sister go.

"Ladies," I said as I landed on their roof, putting Kaylee down beside me.

"Hello, Percival," said Sasha, hand out. "We've come to talk."

"Forgive me if I have my doubts, but your people don't seem to be doing much talking."

They looked at each other, and there was a whole conversation there I wasn't privy to.

"We know," said Greta. "Most of them don't talk. There are a few of us who do, and who have decided that this—"

"It's too much! Fighting enemies is one thing, but this is wholesale slaughter. It's wrong," Sasha spat.

"You're turning on him?"

"*He* turned on *us*," Greta corrected. "He's leaving, leaving us here with what is going to be a slaughter of our people. Yours aren't going to let this go. They're going to scour the tunnels as much as they can, killing every one of us they come across when this is over, and we all know it. More than that, though, he broke his promise. This isn't a better world at all; it's so much worse."

"Wait, leaving?" I asked, shocked.

"He found some other city, Lithere. From what I hear, the tunnels there are extensive, enough that he'll be impossible to dig out."

Lithere was the capital of our country, and while I'd never seen it, I'd heard stories. It had an underground that was legend, a city built upon a city, built upon a city a hundred times over. If half the stories were true, magic had to be involved, as the whole place was described as basically Swiss cheese. If he made it there, he would be entrenched in a way that wasn't possible here.

"That's not possible. He'd either have to take a boat, which he'd never manage without people noticing, or—"

"Or he'd take a portal. There's one near the duke's palace, is there not?" Sasha pointed out. "It's public knowledge."

"I need to go, now."

"Wait, I know you're rushed, but our people need help too." Sasha pointed out. "Sure, some of them are guilty, but some aren't. We need a way to keep the innocent safe."

I hesitated, unsure of what I could do here. Honestly, I had no real power on my own, but I could make introductions.

"That's beyond my reach," I admitted, and they seemed to shrink visibly, "but I know someone. I can't guarantee that he won't kill or maybe even experiment on you, but he works for the duke, and I can put in a good word. Trying to speak with him might be the best you can manage."

They exchanged glances, seemingly bothered by what I'd said.

"I'll go," Sasha said. "You know where to take our people. If I succeed, I'll come for you."

The other girl gave me a long look through her many lenses. "Take care of her as best you can."

"I will," I promised, but that didn't mean much.

Sasha left us, her sister reaching out a hand and touching my shoulder. There was a pop and a slamming wave of agony, and then everything felt right once more. Experimentally, I opened and closed my hand, moving the arm up and down a bit.

"Thanks."

"Of course," she replied. "Now, if you don't mind."

"Right, let's go."

She got in position to run, but I picked both her and Kaylee up; it would be much faster this way. The two girls looked across at each other but said nothing. Whether it was because they didn't know what to say or had some form of enmity, I didn't know and didn't need to. I rushed along, for there really was no time to waste. As soon as I'd started, I had to stop. Behind us, a whole block of the city was being sucked in, seeming to collapse upon itself before exploding like a bomb. My heart sank as it struck me where that had been. My father must have been there, and there was no way he could have survived. Even blocks away, pieces of masonry and flaming rubble began to rain down from the sky. Kaylee made a shield with her bracelet that blocked most of it, and I wanted to stop and stare. I couldn't though. There was still too much to do, and if I let my father's sacrifice go to waste, what sort of son would I be?

No, I needed to get Kaylee to safety. I needed to stop this monster that had called this death upon us. Once and for all.

CHAPTER 46

★

DELIVERING THE NEWS

"Greetings," Ignus said, meeting us at the entryway to the duke's palace. He didn't look particularly pleased.

"Good day," I said. "Before we continue, could you please ask your men to lower their weapons."

Behind the leader of the duke's investigative squad stood a full squadron of men, all angry looking, all pointing various rifles in the direction of my small companion. Behind them were men who could only be magically empowered soldiers, looking no less unhappy about the whole situation.

"I do hope you understand why that's not going to happen, young Percival. Though I'm quite curious as to why you brought this . . . individual here."

"My name is Sasha, and I'm not here to fight you," she said. "A number of us disagree with the current attack and would like to discuss . . . well, what we can do."

He sighed, scratching his head. "You've put me in a bit of a bind here, you see. I'm willing to hear you out, miss, but you'll need to surrender to us. Do that, and it will certainly help."

That was not a promise of any sort, but Sasha didn't seem to care, surrendering to them with a simple nod.

"There are things we need to discuss urgently," she said as the men moved forward to surround her.

"Indeed, let me show the young lord here to his family, and I'll be right with you."

A pair of men took the goblin by the arms and led her not inside the palace, but to the side. That set off alarm bells in my head, but I held my tongue for now, not wanting to make things worse.

"With me," Ignus said, turning and heading into the building.

As we moved inside, I turned to him, frowning. "If you're going to have her shot, you could've at least dropped the deception."

Without breaking his stride the man said, "I'm not, at least not yet. I really do want to hear what she has to say, but that one is the priestess, is she not? Do you know the damage they can do? Have you ever seen it first hand? I have, and let me tell you, boy, that even if she is genuine and the duke accepts, I won't be letting her anywhere near him."

Kaylee had said nothing so far, trying to fade into the background like she'd been taught, but what he'd just said seemed to make her stir.

"You shouldn't speak to him like that," she objected.

"Miss, while I understand you might find some kinship with this boy who saved you, I have a job to do. So I would ask you to keep out of it." He then turned to me. "Now, I don't suppose you know what caused that explosion earlier?"

"I have suspicions, but not confirmation. I would speak to His Grace if possible, for there is much that I need to tell him, and it is urgent."

Ignus regarded me for a few moments, his steps still leading us through the lushly carpeted halls. We'd made it past the entryway now and into the castle proper, art displayed upon the walls. I didn't know this place well, but it was clear we were getting deeper into the duke's domain.

"Normally, I'd hesitate to allow that, but seeing as you brought us a potentially willing source of information, and have proven yourself useful time and again, I'll ask him."

"Thank you," I said. "Sasha had a few things to say, and my father gave us a letter. He seemed insistent that it make it to the duke's hands."

"I don't suppose you know what it says?"

"No, the seal is unbroken."

He led us on, and as we crossed into a hallway with small windows on one side, I heard a series of shots. A quick look through the glass confirmed what I suspected. Several goblins had made their way here, charging toward the building as if to continue their rampage into the castle. Soldiers had dispatched them with extreme prejudice, a mixture of spells, bullets, and armed men ready to meet the assault from every side.

My sister looked out one of the windows but quickly turned around because she couldn't bear to look at the bodies. I'd become almost numb to it, having seen a lot of death in this world, but her? No, Kaylee had never seen one of those things ripped to shreds, and they were very human-like. It was as natural as anything for her to be bothered by it; anyone should be.

"It's okay," I told her as gently as I could, patting her shoulder.

"No, it's horrid, but it will be okay," she replied.

Soon enough, we'd reached the office I'd found myself in once before. With a look that told us we'd regret it if we moved, Ignus slipped inside. As he did I could hear talking, reports being given. When the door shut, though, it all went away, some magical effect enforcing privacy, it seemed, but limited in some way.

Moments passed, and my sister and I smiled at each other. We were stuck here, waiting. I didn't like it, not in the least, but she didn't seem bothered. Had this been how she felt all the time, stuck on the outside while other, more powerful people made decisions she'd have to live with?

"How are you?" I asked.

"I'm . . . odd. I think something is going on with my eyes."

"What do you mean?"

"Well, there are . . . weird shapes and colors all over the place, around people sometimes, and I feel sort of . . . odd? I'm not really sure how to describe it."

"Shapes and colors?"

"Yes, you're surrounded by bubbles. Isn't that strange?"

That was an aura, my aura. I'd met my fair share of casters over my lifetime, and that was always how they'd described it—odd bubbles, a rather unique-looking aura, if there was one. That in and of itself wasn't too strange, though, as everyone was a little different.

"Um . . . how about your mana?" I asked.

"It's fine."

"Even after all that magic?"

She thought for a moment, and then blinked and looked down at her hand. With a look of concentration that made her brows furrow adorably she brought up a pointer finger and made a tiny flame dance around it.

"It doesn't feel like I'm even using it," she said. "How odd."

"You've unlocked your magic; at least I think you have," I informed her, almost laughing. "You're a wizard, Kaylee."

"What?" Her confusion at the strange wording made her lose concentration, the little fire winking out. However, I could see her eyes growing as it began to register.

"Don't worry about it."

It was about this time that Ignus returned, motioning us in. He wasn't alone. Duke Noct had several men and women with him, all surrounded by paperwork.

"I'm told you have a letter for me?" he asked without preamble.

I quickly pulled the sealed envelope from my coat and passed it over. "Father said to give it to you, and that you'd know what to do.

While I have you, the goblin you took into custody and one of her fellows told us of some disturbing plans—"

"It's paperwork for legitimizing a girl named Kaylee," the older man said. "Signed and sealed, important to be sure, but unrelated."

There was a small gasp behind me, this having apparently been one shock too many for my younger half-sister, who almost dropped, knees shaking.

"One moment," I said as I helped her to a nearby couch.

"Miss Kaylee, or rather Lady Kaylee, I presume?" the duke asked.

"Yes," she answered squeakily, "Your Grace."

"Lovely, but not what we need."

"Sorry," I replied. "The girl you took into custody . . . She and another were telling us that their leader means to go to the capital, to insert himself into the underground there."

The soundproofing enchantment only worked one way. I wasn't the only one who heard the series of explosions as I spoke, causing panic throughout the room.

CHAPTER 47

✱

PORTALS

"Another strike?" one of the men nearby asked.

"Much closer than the previous ones. That way?" I told them, pointing.

For a moment I saw the duke pale, eyes following my hand. "The portal nexus is that way."

"Well, sounds like they won," someone said.

"The leader of the goblins is a death priest. That much is known." Ignus didn't hold back, making the whole room fall deadly silent.

"I'll go," I said.

"No, one of my people will go," Ignus insisted. "You know these creatures best, and we cannot risk you at this moment."

Before I could argue, he popped into the hall and ran, seemingly searching for the right people.

Within the room, though, the silence was grating. Nobody knew what to say or what to do. It held for moments, and we could all hear that the noise from outside had died down. Then the duke himself broke it.

"The gates have safety measures; there's little reason to worry."

"If they fail, if he gets into the capital, who knows how many could die in the fighting."

"He won't make it to the capital. No publicly accessible portal goes directly there, hasn't in over a century. Military ones, perhaps, but we don't have one of those at this facility. Those goblins would have to survive leaving here, and then get from the nexus to one of the Central Duchies. From there some further transport."

"The what?"

"Ah," Duke Noct laughed. "Nobody uses the term anymore. The capital is surrounded by duchies called the Central Duchies. An old form of address, but they form the whole central region of the country."

"I see. Ignus will be here momentarily." I could hear him in the hall, running back toward us.

"They blitzed the guards," Ignus announced as he entered. "About half made it through before the emergency measures took effect, but they're moving. We need to contact the king now and alert him to what is coming, see if we can get more information."

"Can we follow?" I asked.

"No, not for at least half an hour," Ignus said, "and that is if the other side attempts to reestablish contact. Procedures are pretty sticky, and we'll need to see what's happening."

"Percival, I appreciate your work so far, but what comes next is state secrets you are not privy to, nor shall you be for some time. Please follow my aide here, and he will show you to your family." Duke Noct spoke kindly but firmly, and though it stung, he was right. I wasn't privy to a lot of things, and there was little help I could be for now.

"Very well, Your Grace. Should you need anything I can provide, please let me know. I'm more than happy to help." He nodded, and I gathered my sister before doing as he bade me.

Kaylee, for her part, seemed to be in shock, and that wasn't surprising at all. She'd been through a lot today. Truly, we all had, and it was proving to be too much for her to process at the moment. Did I worry? No, she was a smart girl, and dedicated. She'd get through this fine, eventually.

My family, along with some of our closest servants were in a room deep in the castle. As the door opened I could see Mother pacing, stress written upon her face. Both sets of my grandparents were here, as well, and they looked bothered too. My two grandfathers holding themselves still, but too still, faces furrowed and dark. As for my grandmothers, they looked to be trying to calm Mother, both near her, but at a careful distance.

"Percival!" she all but shouted when she saw me, blinking across the room faster than I'd ever seen her move and wrapping me in a tight hug.

"Fool boy, what in the world were you thinking! Where's your father? I've half a mind to give him a good beating!"

My silence hung heavy in the air, and when she finally pulled back to look at me, I shook my head slowly. She froze, all the anger leaving her in an instant, eyes disbelieving.

"Where, son? What happened?" she stammered.

"He rescued us, and he was better than I've ever seen him before, told us to leave. Mother, the explosion was close, and the way he spoke . . . he knew he wasn't coming back."

"But you didn't see it?"

"No . . ."

"So maybe, maybe he's okay, just hiding, or buried. We need to send someone to go and find him immediately!" she nearly screamed as she turned toward the aide, starting to move.

I stopped her with a hand. She was strong, but over the years I'd gotten stronger. "Mother, stop."

"But he's still out there; what are you doing!" Her shrill voice made the aide grimace as he backed toward the door, knowing full well this was not a good moment.

"Enough!" The one word I shouted was all it took to stop her and draw her eyes to me once again.

Acceptance of the truth hit her like a blow. Her muscles, only moments ago struggling to go, struggling to get someone to do something, went limp as tears began to fall. She stumbled, and I had to help her over to the nearest couch. My grandmothers moved to her side, whispering calming words. My grandfather, the ever unflappable Baron Shadestone, closed his eyes. To most of the people here it would seem as if he were silently waiting, but I could hear it. His teeth grinding and fist clenched; and I could see the muscles on his face tighten as he schooled himself before coming over and putting a hand on my shoulder. My father may have been an absolute mess, but he was still his son.

"I heard about what you did today, son, and I'm proud of you," he told me with a slight squeeze.

All through the castle people were talking, holding one another, and reassuring each other. The atmosphere was heavy, with tears and people shaking from fear or stress. Men and women embraced trying to make sure their loved ones were all right.

And the city outside? It was chaos. Pockets of fighting remained, with men wielding whatever they could use as weapons against the horde, while others huddled in terror in their homes, praying for rescue. Soldiers and officers began to gather in groups, going street to street, house to house, room to room, looking for enemies and survivors, each face a rictus of fury when they found one of the former.

Hundreds lay dead in the streets, thousands more were injured, and soon there would be fury unlike any had known. It took time to fully mobilize fighters, particularly when they were so surprised, but soon, very soon, the city would be scoured, and woe to those who'd brought this calamity upon us.

CHAPTER 48

✶

BIG REVEAL

Time seemed to slow to a crawl. There was nothing we could do, nowhere to go, and other than comforting each other, there was no action we could take that would accomplish anything at all. My grandfathers were too old to join the fight, and I too young to volunteer. The ladies, of course, weren't expected to join, so we all just stayed here.

Mother had settled upon a couch and was deep in her grief. In time I knew she'd get past it, but for now she needed to grieve. I spent a few moments with her, but my grandmothers had done better than I could, and there were other things I needed to discuss anyway.

Moving to Grandpa's side, I could tell he was feeling down. He might not have been my father's biggest fan, but he could tell that the death had caused pain. Grandfather Shadestone sat near him, the two of them discussing what resources each could bring if and when they were called to action.

"I've still a few contacts with the military, so we might be able to . . ." the baron explained as I joined.

"We might need to deploy the plane for reconnaissance," I told them, poking my head in, knowing they'd not discussed this option.

"It would be useful, but I'm unsure where Lionel is, and without him . . ." Grandpa Darksky had apparently thought of that already, but it seemed our test pilot was nowhere to be found currently.

"Without him we'll have to fly it, which we're both perfectly capable of," I retorted. "We both know how, and it would be no problem at all for either of us."

"How long would it take to get it?" asked Grandfather.

"Twenty minutes on fast steeds, assuming we don't run into any snags along the way. If Percival ran or I flew, perhaps fifteen to get out of the city and to the storehouse where it is kept."

"And to bring it back here?"

"Fifteen tops," I answered, knowing how fast that thing could travel if needed.

"I didn't know you could fly," I told Grandpa.

"Haven't in years," he replied. "The experience is . . . unpleasant and extremely mana intensive. There are a few who've mastered it, but for me it's more like hurling yourself through the sky."

As we continued discussing the issue, a sound reached my ears that I could not and would not ignore.

"I know you've been through much, but get up this instant. I will not tolerate such rudeness," the low voice of our housekeeper, Mrs. Rider, said with an angry hiss.

Kaylee had settled on a small couch in the corner of the room, well away from anyone else. She was still in her maid uniform and looking absently into the ether. I should've said something before, but I'd not wanted to bring it up, and then I'd forgotten with all that was going on.

Now the housekeeper loomed over her, clearly angry at the girl for just sitting there. Maids, and staff in general, weren't permitted to sit when their employers were around, and so her seated position could be taken as a severe insult. The family had been too deep in our own problems to even look that way, but Mrs. Rider had, and it seemed she'd taken deep offense.

Interestingly, I was taking deep offense, too, but to someone else.

"My sister may sit wherever she pleases," I said before her bottom could so much as leave the couch, loud enough that all here could hear it, and with steel in my words. It might not have been the best way to put this information forward, but there wasn't another time. I couldn't have her disrespected now that she'd been acknowledged, and I wouldn't. The room went dead silent, enough to hear a pin drop. As for Mrs. Rider, she froze in place, looking like someone had hit her with a cattle prod, before turning to me and finding my eyes locked on hers.

"Percival, what nonsense are you saying?" Mother asked, pushing the other women off and moving to stand.

I sighed. "The last thing Father did was embrace the both of us and give me the paperwork acknowledging Kaylee. It has already been handed over to His Grace."

To say that that comment caused a bit of an uproar might have been an understatement.

"I can't believe you would lie!"

"Calm down!"

"Of all the things!"

"SILENCE!" Grandpa Shadestone roared, loud enough that all other conversation died. "Percival, is this true?"

"It is," I confirmed.

"I see."

"Percival, y-you don't look surprised in the least," Mother observed.

"No, I'm not."

"You knew... How long have you known?"

"Basically since I was born," I admitted.

"Did others know?" Her eyes flicked toward the baron, who didn't move, but was clearly keeping his face straight. Then she looked toward her mother-in-law, who didn't even bother to meet her eyes. "Am I the only one who didn't know my husband had an affair!?"

"Not everyone," I assured her, but that didn't make her any happier.

"Well then," her eyes went to Kaylee, who tried to disappear into her seat. "We'll have to change some things, I suppose."

"Mother," I warned, narrowing my eyes.

"Enough, son, I'm not going to hurt the girl. Would've liked to beat your father though."

"If it helps, I did end up in conflict with him about it a while back; I nearly stabbed him."

"It does not. As for the moment, I don't know."

"Well, I'll take things then," the baroness declared, rising and going over to the scared-looking Kaylee. "Come, dear, we can't well have you around in that outfit. Imagine the confusion."

With a kind but firm hand, my grandmother took Kaylee from the room. I imagined they'd be having a very long conversation, and that there'd definitely be fallout for Mrs. Lutte. We would need to send her a letter later, but Grandmother seemed to have things well in hand for the moment.

Before we could fully settle back down, Ignus knocked on the door, and when he stepped inside, the man was clearly stressed and worried.

"Ah, there you are, just the fellows I need. Percival, I'd like to consult with you and your grandpa, if that's all right."

CHAPTER 49

✱

EMERGENCY TAKEOFF

"What's going on," I asked as we escorted Ignus into the hall.

"The short version is this: They made it through the portal and managed to escape the fortress on the far side. I'm still unsure how they knew, but the gate was scheduled to open so the people on the far end didn't immediately sound a full alert, an error on our part. It was enough, and those goblins made it through to another city."

"Going where?" Grandpa inquired.

"I'll let His Grace give you the full details," he told us as he opened the door to the office.

"Please tell us everything we need to know," I requested.

"That death priest made it to one of the duchies, not the nearest to the capital, thank goodness, but one near enough. He's also managed to take a train, loaded with passengers."

"Well, the king's men need to do something then," Grandpa put forth.

"They are," the duke responded. "They know they can't risk that train making it to the capital, and the danger if it does."

"So what, they'll send knights to board it and slaughter the beasts?" I asked.

"No, it is going too fast for that to be reliable. By the time proper forces can be arrayed, it will be too late. His Majesty has weighed the options and made his decision. The train will be derailed, about half an hour outside the city in a place where they can bombard it until nothing remains."

"The passengers and crew though," I pointed out.

"Aren't as important as protecting the city. It is a difficult decision, but the kind that leaders must make."

"They'll be sacrificed," I mumbled.

"Unless someone can get to them and kill the goblins in time. However, you'd need something fast and agile to overtake the train, and coming at a speed and from a direction none could anticipate."

"Does the king know of this?" Grandpa asked.

"Specifically? No, but he did tell me to do what I could. This is that, is it not? Can you do it?"

"How much time to we have?" I asked.

"Three hours at most."

"Then we need to leave now."

"I cannot seriously believe you're considering this," Grandpa Darksky complained, his pointed ears moving as he listened to our words.

"I'm going either way," I said. "Are you with me or not?" I asked.

"Very well." With that, he moved to the window behind the duke. "We're going my way though. Your Grace, please have the gate ready for us, along with maps. We'll need them if this farce is to have any chance."

I moved behind him and felt chains of force wrap themselves around me. Sure, I could've resisted, but this seemed to be part of his plan, and what a plan it was. With a movement of his hands he flung us out the window.

He'd called this flight, stating that it wasn't a good way but something he could do, and I had to agree. It was a terrible way to fly, and nothing like the flight our machine could achieve. Instead, Grandpa basically flung himself forward like a missile, dragging me along. The pull was uneven, letting us drop at times before slamming back into me. The wildest rollercoasters from Earth would've been envious at the nausea this particular ride induced, hurling me this way and that.

"This is a disaster," I complained as we were tossed through the sky over the city.

"Better than it used to be," he remarked. "Now silence yourself; it isn't easy."

Below us I could see people moving through the lanes where traffic once moved. Groups of men faced off against factions of the little green beasts, hacking and shooting where they could. Around the palace, there were formations of soldiers beginning to spread, moving between buildings in professional lines, but they were outnumbered by the mobs defending their homes three to one.

The defenders weren't fully successful, though, and in certain places it was clear to see that things weren't going well. Entire buildings were ablaze, flames licking at the stone or brick shells as they consumed the insides. Bodies lay sprawled in puddles of blood, and wrecked carriages and dead horses lay where they'd been felled, splintered and broken like children's toys.

Finally, we passed over my childhood home, or what it was now. The whole block was nothing but a crater, littered with broken masonry and shattered wood. A circle had been cut in the earth, everything collapsed within it, hundreds of feet wide and full of nothing but debris. Even around it there were fallen buildings, structures that couldn't survive the explosion that had followed the initial strike. Those still standing bore scars across their facades, one whole side of them peppered and blasted apart.

Grandpa said nothing as we passed over the place I'd grown up. No more were the familiar rooms lined with trophies and knickknacks. Gone were the halls I'd frequented since I was a baby, the hidden hallways and backrooms now reduced to nothing. Even the streets I'd known since I was a child were torn apart and cast aside like they had never been.

Somewhere down there was what was left of my father, assuming anything at all remained. We'd need to look when this was over, try to find some piece of him and give him a proper burial. That would all come later though. Now we needed to put an end to the man who should've ended years ago and worlds away. If nothing else, that could serve as a memorial to my father.

We made better time than Grandpa had initially estimated, arriving perhaps ten minutes after leaving the palace. With a thud we slammed into the field outside our makeshift hangar, and though I was disoriented, I sped toward the doors. With quick movements I threw them open, revealing our noble steed.

The plane we'd spent years perfecting—sourcing the materials, building, and testing—stood silent, ready. I made it to the cockpit first and began the preflight checks. The magical engine was full and ready. I did a once-over, and everything looked perfect, ready—ready to do what it needed.

"Ready?" my grandpa asked.

"As we can be," I responded as he settled into his seat behind me. I tossed the throttle forward, silently pulling us out of the shaded hangar and into the light.

CHAPTER 50

★

EXITING EXION

Our plane ate the miles as fast as Grandpa's magical flight had, and significantly more comfortably. It seemed one moment we were in the hangar and the next we were over the city, looking for our landing place. The men there had been kind enough to lay one out for us, right next to the building where I assumed the portal lay, one I'd never been through before.

Lights guided us in, pulling up right at the large entrance to what could itself have been another fortress. People weren't stupid. Every single portal had some form of protection around it. That was for good reason—worries about the very thing that was happening right now. If soldiers could move from one place to another quickly and infiltrate targets with ease, the damage they could do was astronomical. We'd gotten lax, though, and our current situation demonstrated it too clearly.

The doors to the portal fortress were massive, easily large enough for a carriage to pass through. That, of course, made sense, since these were sometimes used to transport large shipments that absolutely needed to be retrieved immediately. There was also no short supply of wealthy individuals and others who wanted to bring cargo with them. It was expensive, but it was the fastest way to travel.

"Do we have any information?" I asked as we landed and began to remove the wings; as big as it was, this was something that needed to be done. It wasn't a problem, as it was designed for this in the original plans—shipping and all.

"I'll get Mr. Ignus," said the soldier who'd guided us in, turning and running to the doors.

The man in question met him halfway, another in tow. "Allow me to introduce my colleague; we have some things for you."

"Please don't mind us," Grandpa responded, undoing bolts almost as fast as I was. "We're quite eager to hear it."

"We counted nine total that made it through, led by the death priest. They're well ahead of you, but if this contraption is fast enough, you might just have a chance to catch them. Keep in mind that royal soldiers are preparing to intercept, as well, and you certainly do not want to be between the two forces when they do. I've also the maps here for review. The train lines have been outlined in red, along with the most likely heading to cut down what you can before following the tracks."

"Other magic users or physicals?" I asked as I lifted and began turning the whole apparatus.

"Unknown, but we don't think so. If they are, they didn't use any." The man seemed stressed and hadn't even given his name, not that I needed that.

"Odd, more odd that he left some of his best here too," I mused.

"I've also talked to your friend, Miss Sasha, and my conclusion is this," Ignus began. "He was getting push-back. The girls knew what he was up to and disapproved, making their stances known. There's also that big one she mentioned, her brother. He seemed unstable, stupid, violent, the whole package really. Between that and the obvious attack here, I think he's abandoning Exion completely. None of the goblins here are meant to live."

"Cold," I replied as maps were handed to me, and I began to read as we walked the plane toward the portal.

"Death priest," Ignus said. "I've only heard rumors because of how damn rare they are, but from what I've read, they justify everything to themselves. All deaths are for the greater good, every betrayal is to help others, to help the whole world; and they believe it too. It's why they're so dangerous. A normal priest betraying their fellows would get weaker by bounds, their magic inhibited, but he thinks he's doing right, so it only makes him stronger."

Ignus' observations worried me.

"So he took only those he knew he could control," I said. "Excellent."

"Has Mr. Lionel been found?" my grandpa asked as we approached the building.

"I'm afraid not," Ignus responded. "Why?"

"I do not wish my grandson to be going anywhere near this."

"There's no other choice, Grandpa. If anything goes wrong with the plane, we'll need two, and there are only two seats. We've only got one chance at saving these lives."

"A fact of which I'm acutely aware, but that doesn't mean I like it."

It was the truth, and we both knew it. If there were any problems with the plane's magic, he'd need to be there to fix them; he knew more about that system than anyone. Similarly, I knew more about the moving parts and the physics than anyone else around and was the only one of the two of us who'd ever flown, if just the once.

The hall was straight and filled with men, the portal already going. The light, a pale blue swirl, was unlike anything I'd seen before, and it shocked me. It looked like something from a TV show or a movie. Among the running men I saw my headmaster, the beast of a man, approaching to walk with us as we moved closer to the glowing hole in space.

"You have your weapons, Percival?"

"Yes, sir," I said, patting my pistol and sword cane.

"That one won't do. Good for defense, but not a weapon of war." His eyes lingered on the cane briefly.

"Don't have time to get another one."

He gave me a hard look and nodded, and then his hand went to his own belt. The sword that hung there was a bit larger than I was used to and resembled the practice staffs we had around the school.

"This was a gift, and I expect you to return it," he said as he passed over the blade, sheath and all. "It will cut steel like paper and through men without issue, so use care."

We both stopped for a second. He hadn't asked to come along. He had probably seen how many seats there were in the plane. I extended my cane to him.

"This was a gift, too, sir. Please look after it until I return," I told him as he took my blade.

"Good man," he told me as our group stepped through the portal.

CHAPTER 51

✶

RESCUE BEGINS

It took only minutes for the plane to be back in working order, and I looked at our runway.

"It's short," Grandpa said.

"It's what we have, and it should be long enough," I replied; but he was right, it was shorter than I'd have liked.

"We go then?"

"We go."

Things were worse here than I could've feared. The people here had been caught just as unprepared, and Father—no, Parkov—hadn't held back. He and his group had slaughtered dozens and dozens, bodies laid out in rows. Now it was our time to take him down.

Grandpa gunned it, and we sped down the road that was our only runway. Feet sped by around us, shopfronts appearing and disappearing as we went faster and faster, until I finally felt the wheels leave the ground. Just in time, too, as we barely cleared the roof of an old inn, a mermaid sign hanging over its door.

Higher and higher we climbed, needing to see to get our bearings properly and orient via the maps we'd been given. Exion was massive, but this city was on another level entirely, making my home look like a small town in comparison. It was old, too, lacking the more grid-like layout of the island city and following more organic paths instead, grids only appearing in the outer sections of the settlement.

There was no time to waste. Once we had our bearings we set off. Finding the train station was easy enough, and the tracks that led off from it not much harder. Even then we didn't follow it exactly. This particular train had been made early on and wasn't particularly straight, curving a bit around hills and valleys carved into the landscape. We had no need to do so, instead pulling ahead to where it would be.

"We should've seen it by now!" Grandpa shouted over the wind.

He was right. Trains only went so fast, so where was it? My eyes followed the track, and soon I saw a cloud of steam in the distance, a few miles ahead.

"They're going fast!" I said. "We need to do the same to catch up!"

That worried me. This plane was only designed for short flights, and not for speed, but Grandpa didn't flinch, pushing us forward even faster. For a moment I worried, knowing that we were going to be at the upper end of our range with all these flights, but one look at the gauges told me that we had no issue at all. The amount of mana left in our engine wasn't full, but it was far higher than I might have expected.

"We're using less mana!" I told him, the roar of the air taking my words.

"No, you fool boy! I'm feeding it. Now hold on!"

We closed in, a silent falcon slowly approaching its prey from behind, ready to strike. Their billowing steam clouds hid our approach as much as they could, and the fact that we were silent meant they'd have no warning.

As our plane got close enough, I shoved myself out of my seat, holding on with all my strength and scooted forward, speaking in Grandpa's ear.

"Provide me air support," I said. "Keep the plane close, and once I've cleared a car, I'll cut it free from the train. None of them escape." He nodded at my words and pulled us as close as sanity allowed.

A boy sat in the back of the train, and as we neared, I saw his eyes widen in shock. His face, streaked with tears, blinked at me. How strange we must look, an old man and a boy who was barely a man, flying behind them on a craft he'd never even imagined. I met his eyes, nodded, smiled, and leapt forward with sword in hand and ready for battle.

Ten feet had never felt further. A leap so small was something I could practically do in my sleep, but with the wind whipping at my coat and hair and the roar of the wheels on the track, it felt so far to the ground that flowed below us, like it wasn't even real.

I didn't even land before my blade began to move. The headmaster had claimed it could cut steel like paper, and it was time to test that out, for I didn't want anyone warning the other goblins that I had arrived before I had a chance to begin. My borrowed blade arced up and through the door before me an instant before my foot landed on the railing behind it, and I catapulted forward.

"Mommy!" I heard the boy cry out as I blasted through the doorway, taking in the scene as quickly as I could.

All along the train car men and women were sitting, scared, and they pulled back, while in the aisle stood a green humanoid, looking toward the front. There was only one enemy here, so I kept on with my charge, feet slamming down as fast as I could work them. He didn't even have time to turn before I reached him, a flash of steel separating his head from his body before he even realized I'd begun.

There was a collective gasp around me as time returned to normal. A goblin head thunked upon the floor before a spray of blood blasted across the aisle, pumping as the creature's heart kept going for a few seconds, trying to keep him alive.

I looked down at my enemy, and he was different. More human, less bestial, and the ears. All goblins had slightly pointed ears, but his were ... more, the shape different, more graceful, more ... elven. That was bad. That was very, very bad. With makeup on his skin, he could have passed for human even, or at least a partly elven human.

"Are there others in this car?" I asked, seeing none myself but not foolish enough to think I knew better.

"I-I sir, there, but—" a woman stammered.

"Answer quickly, for time is of the essence," I pressed, trying to be firm but not too harsh.

"No, sir, just the one."

I didn't speak again, nor did I give the rest of the car time to panic as I sped toward the far doorway, the connector between this car and the next. One door opened, then closed behind me, and I looked at the connections. They were rather thorough with these—a large metal hooking mechanism between the cars and backup chains hanging all around it, just to make sure. I had to hope the sword would cut these as easily as it had the doorway.

With wide sweeps I slashed through the chains, and then, with some trepidation and both hands, I tried my luck with the connector. The results convinced me I needed one of these, as true to the advertisement, it hardly slowed down, feeling almost natural as a near foot-thick section of steel parted, a clean slice through it.

"One down," I declared, as friction began to slowly pull the caboose away, eyes looking forward to me from inside as mouths began to shout. If nothing else, I'd managed to save at least those people. Now for the rest of them.

CHAPTER 52

✶

CHILDREN AT WAR

The train lurched as the first of the cars fell away. That had not been intended, nor was it welcome in the least. Had I known . . . no, I probably still would have cut the car away, no need to expose those people to any further risk.

It did, however, make the people in the car before me scream and look about in panic as I entered from the back.

"Is anyone hurt?" I asked as I strode in, looking for enemies and finding none.

My question was answered before anyone spoke. On one of the seats was a man, bleeding profusely from a wound to his gut, the slash covered with cloth and tied tight, but it wasn't stopping. It was a nasty injury. On Earth it might well have been a slow way to die. If he didn't get to someone to aid him soon, he certainly would. A risk, but I had to leave him behind.

"Tried to stop them, but . . ." he began, grey hairs sticking to his forehead from the sweat.

"Everything will be all right. I'm here to help," I told him.

"Where's the rest of your team?" the elderly woman beside him asked, worriedly.

"Not here at the moment, but worry not, help will be here before long." I didn't bother telling them that help was a pretty loose definition, and we might soon have soldiers trying to destroy the train outright. They didn't need that kind of stress.

A few people seemed a bit put off by that answer, maybe seeing the deflection.

"What do we do?" a little girl asked, still clearly afraid.

"Sit tight, I'll take care of it," I reassured her.

We'd heard there were nine goblins total. With one down, that meant eight more to go, and I didn't have time to waste. I made my way to the opening between cars once more, but before I could cut the primary connection, there was a scream of rage.

I turned in time to see her, for it was decidedly a her, making a throwing motion toward me. Instinct took over, and I ducked under what looked like a ball of lightning. It slammed through the window, letting people see the other cars and melting the glass. It struck the car I'd just left, sending a wave of energy out that even through my resistance made my skin tingle.

That attack against anyone else would be quite deadly, more than what I'd seen from the other goblins. All the people inside the cars should be fine, for the same reason that you'd be okay if lightning hit your car—they were basically sitting inside faraday cages. Nor was her attack that much a problem for me. My resistance to magic should protect me, not that I wanted to get hit.

However, she didn't follow up with another blow. Interesting. Either she was waiting for something, or she couldn't. As the door to the car she was in slammed open, and before she had a chance to do anything, I put my blade through her. As her face realized that there was now a sword piercing her chest, I saw that she was young. Not just young, but almost childlike. If she'd been a human, perhaps fourteen, maybe fifteen? Thinking back, the other one was like that too. I was effectively fighting children. Even though I was in the body of a very young man, that struck me.

I had no choice though. Two down, seven to go.

After cutting the previous car away, I moved ahead again. People called out to me, but there really was no time. The train shook with each one I released, and I noticed something else. We were moving faster. As I cut away the weights, it had less pulling it back.

One car with nothing, then I saw the next. The goblin there was bulkier, with a large metal club, like the ones Japanese demons were always depicted with. He was kind enough to let me actually enter before doing anything. This was a dining car, too, with no people; it was just the two of us, tables, chairs, and a bar.

"What you doing?" he asked.

"Saving these people," I responded. "If you surrender, I'll do what I can for you too."

"No, Father save these people," he replied. "You a danger and have to go. No hard feelings." His grammar was poor, but he did at least sound like he didn't hate me.

We both charged, and I was surprised. The initial attack looked like it was simple, an attempt to crush, but before the clash, his weapon turned, striking the flat of my sword and slamming it hard enough that it flew from my hand.

For an instant I felt panic. I watched as he raised his club again, ready to kill me. With nothing to meet his strike, I wasn't in a good position, but there were options. I charged, moving too close for him to get his weapon swinging again and began to punch. It seemed counterintuitive but was something our classes had taught us to keep the enemy from generating any power with their weapons, and here it would work. There was no time for anything else.

My face was inches from him as I tried to land blows anywhere I could in quick succession. Kidney, stomach. Getting a shot at his solar plexus would be perfect, but I couldn't get the angle right. Before we reached the floor, though, he used the pommel of his weapon to slam me in the side, sending me sprawling over the nearby bar.

As I hit the floor I rolled, reaching for the pistol at my waist now that I had room. Just in time, too, as the club came down where I'd landed a second earlier, sending broken glass and liquor everywhere. I popped up, aiming quickly and pulling the trigger.

Once more my opponent used his club, bringing it before his body as I aimed and sending the bullet ricocheting, bringing his club around again. Once more I dove, firing off another shot as he took off all the taps on the bar and much of the display case behind it with a sweeping gesture.

"You're pretty good," I said as I rolled out and hopped over a table.

"You too," he replied as he wrecked the small wooden barrier.

A kick sent a chair flying at his face and he flinched. Whoever this goblin was, he had skill and potential, but nowhere near enough training. He was young, just like the others. That flinch allowed me to put two rounds in his center of mass.

I thought it was over, but no such luck. He moved forward this time, but his charge was interrupted as the carriage shook, part of the ceiling being blown away. We looked briefly, seeing two halves of a lithe form flying away into the night, nothing connecting the top and bottom.

"Cinna?" the goblin said, pain in his voice as his eyes widened in shock. It seemed he'd had a backup plan if he wasn't able to handle me on his own.

It felt dirty, but I took his momentary shock to put a bullet through his eye. I couldn't let the innocents die. His body froze like he'd been shocked, then he fell over, brain destroyed in an instant.

"Sorry, friend," I said to him. "You seemed like a decent sort."

In the sky above I could see the plane, my grandfather sitting in the seat. Much like my enemy, I wasn't alone.

With a sigh I retrieved the sword, happy to see it wasn't damaged. What if we'd managed to get to these goblins before they left? Could Sasha have convinced them not to follow in this madness? Clearly they, too, were victims, children pulled into a war they couldn't possibly understand.

There was no time for consideration though. Instead, I set my jaw, took my blade, and moved forward.

Five left to go.

CHAPTER 53

✶

TO FINISH IT

There was no wind in my sails for my grim work. I reloaded and moved to the next cart, cutting one more free. I'd considered leaving it, but that was senseless. What if one of the goblins got back in there and hid or did something else foolish? No, it was better for me to make their area smaller and smaller, preventing me from having to deal with any issues from behind. The better option was to take away their places to run, like rats in a trap, then slaughter them.

As for the large one I'd slain, I took a moment to leave a tablecloth over him. Regardless of the fact that we'd been enemies and he'd nearly killed me, he'd been civilized, so he deserved a civilized death. Had he not cared for the other one of his kind, he may well have won, but war was like that. Nobody knew who would die for sure, and nobody knew if they were coming back.

The next car was a kitchen, and here I found another attacker, but not inside it. He saw me coming from the window on the far side, while he was between the cars. What a terror I must have been to him, with blood on my clothing and a blade still slick with the red life of his brother. We locked eyes and he turned, running for his life.

I followed him, pausing only to cut loose the car as he sprinted through the first-class dining car and toward the very front of the train. It seemed on this particular train car they'd set things so that the front-riding passengers and the lower-class ones never needed to meet. It was not uncommon, but it pricked against my sensibilities a bit.

As the last of the food-related cars began to fall back, I moved into the first-class car. It was the same size as the others but seemed more spacious. There were fewer people, of course, with larger areas for each. More expensive tickets, fancier placements.

The people were huddled in a small, cleared space, and there were a total of ten of them. None of them bore the fancy clothing of the aristocracy; nor had they killed these beasts. So, if they had any magic, it wasn't much. Around them were the last four of the lesser goblins, the one who'd run from me, heaving as he approached the other three. Before I could charge, he ripped a girl from her parents and held a blade to her throat.

"Done fleeing?" I asked, tired of this.

Outside, the landscapes flew past, the wheels making angry noises as the vehicle sped to levels it had never been designed for.

"Stop! If you don't, I'll slit her throat! Drop the weapon!" he shouted.

I did not drop my sword.

"Do you know how far this has gone?" I asked.

"I'm not lying!"

Did he even hear me? "Soldiers are coming; they will kill everyone," I told him.

"Wait, hold on!" one of the three shouted to us. I noticed all of them were female; it seemed Father had chosen a large proportion of women for his new nest. "What do you mean?"

"Men are coming," I informed them calmly. "They will kill all of us. They will kill you, they will kill me, they will kill that child. Threatening her changes nothing. She will die, regardless, if I stop.

The only way I can save anyone is to make sure you're not around anymore."

"We need to tell Father," one of the goblin girls said. "He'll know what to do. Listen, human, when he gets here we can talk."

The male flinched.

"Granen, don't do something stupid!" she yelled as the little knife pricked the girl, making a drop of blood roll down her neck. "Wait till we get Father!"

Granen must have been his name, for as she shouted at him he turned to look. It was enough for me, and in one fluid motion I drew my pistol and shot, unable to miss at this distance. I couldn't let them get Father. I couldn't let him plan anything.

Everyone was screaming—the goblins, the terrified child, several of the passengers who thought I'd just killed her. The last three goblins charged, each conjuring a small projectile in their hands, some kind of minor spell. I wasn't alone now though. Some of these men understood that my words hadn't just been for the goblins.

The three goblin girls had thought the passengers cowards, but a man reached out as they turned to me, a burst of ice plastering one into the wall, blood spraying. The spell from another flew wide, a ball of red fire that hit somewhere behind me with a blast of heat. Then came a ball of water, which I cut in two with my sword, shattering the construct before it could do much at all, though I still got quite wet.

Passengers surged over one of the two remaining goblins as I stepped forward, a clean slice taking the head off the other. As for the final one, angry men slammed her into the ground, arms grasped by hands that looked unused to violence.

"No, please!" she screamed, but as she did, I saw another fireball growing in her palm.

I knew it was panic, fear making her cast, but I couldn't risk it. Had she not done that, perhaps I could have spared her. Risky, but perhaps. With her still using magic, though, I had no choice.

Putting aside mercy I brought the point of my blade down, straight through her heart.

"I'm sorry," I whispered.

"Good work, son," one of the men said, clapping me on the shoulder as I stood. I ignored him, not wanting praise for this. It was not some joyous act. It was war. It was brutal, terrible, and full of victims.

But there was also a perpetrator, the one who'd caused all of this.

"Where are you going?" a woman asked shakily as I walked away from the nervous passengers.

"To finish it," I informed her. "There's only one left."

The final cart I passed through was for staff, and full of them. Stewards and stewardesses were laid upon the floor, shaking, seemingly unable to rise.

"H-h-h-h," one of them tried to speak as I walked over her.

"It's going to be okay," I said, hoping to believe it myself. "Help is coming, but I cannot stay."

"W-w-w," his voice trembled, unable to form even a word.

"Stay, it will be fine," I assured again as I moved to the door.

I cut that car away, too, before looking at the engine. It was what was propelling us forward, and where I sensed I would find my enemy, the true enemy, not those he'd thrown against me, but the one who truly deserved my ire.

As calmly as I could I opened the door, stepping inside but leaving it to flap out behind me. It went unnoticed, though, as I could hear shouting from the front.

"We can't go any faster, and we need to slow down, you foolish beast! At this speed, if we hit any kind of curve we'll derail and all die," a man screamed in desperation.

"Not one bit. Keep going; there's been no problem up until now, and I won't hear your lies!" Then I saw him turn, looking back to where I was. "You!"

"Isn't that enough, Parkov?" I asked using his Earth name.

"My children, where are they?"

"You know."

"Monster! They were my greatest creations, and you murdered them? To what end? Surely you know you'll lose."

"The only ones who will survive this are those you left to die. They betrayed you, you know." I had to think for a moment, for perhaps I could save the conductor, too, but more importantly, I had to make sure Parkov died.

I could read the signs here, see the danger. Some of the tools looked almost modern, but some looked cartoonishly old school. The speed control was a lever, pulled to increase or decrease the power to the wheels. Gauges were going crazy, too, showing danger everywhere. I might not have been a train conductor, but I'd been on enough trains and seen enough engine rooms to know that. I saw something else, too, when I looked out the front window. In the far distance soldiers were moving, doing something, trying to stay hidden. We had perhaps a minute, maybe more.

"Foolish, you can't defeat me," Parkov began.

The conductor, in an act of heroism, reached for a wrench. Sadly, the death priest was faster, a pulse of magic making the man fall, blood leaking from his eyes. The same pulse hit me and it hurt, making me fall to my knees.

"Ow," I gasped.

"Ow, indeed. I'm going to kill you now, young man, but first I want you to know. I want you to know that I will survive," he began as he advanced toward me. "I will rebuild, making more children, greater children, and then I'll improve the whole world. You could have joined me, could have been more; but no, you'll die a pathetic, broken fool." He patted his stomach. "I alone am enough."

He reached down, and I threw my hand up, wrapping it around his throat. Another pulse hit me, and it hurt, but I'd learned to deal with magic like this.

"Magic not working like it should?" I asked as I charged forward, slamming him into the speed control handle hard enough to impale him.

"I can survive far more than this!" he hissed as he struggled like a pinned animal.

"Maybe," I said as I looked up, seeing the men who had been sent to stop this moving train, "but not that."

"What?" he asked as he tried to turn, but was unable to.

Mages were calling stone blocks up out of the ground and moving them across the track. More were coming out of the nearby foliage on either side of the train, readying weapons and spells. We were only moments away.

"You know, you can keep the train," I informed him as I bent the handle between two pipes and bolted, running for the door.

"This isn't over!" he screamed as I made my way through the opening, jumping for all I was worth.

It was a strange sensation. The train had been moving at an incredible speed, but so had I. It wasn't like I was really moving much in the direction I'd tried to go, merely bleeding off some of the speed, slowing the rate at which the ground seemed to be pushing past me.

The ground still rose up to meet me at speed, but it was more like being thrown from a horse than from a car. I rolled, dropping the sword I'd not bothered to use on the psychopathic death priest. Three times I bounced, three times until I came to rest, sore, but alive.

A second later, the train's impact echoed across the land, the bending and rending of metal. The screaming as the pipes bent in ways they'd never been made to, and the cabin was crushed. It was followed by a wave of heat and the unmistakable sound of rifle reports. Within me there was a great debate—to look back or not. The part of me that wanted to look cool forbade such an action, screaming that I must resist. Though curiosity ordered me to turn, to watch the literal train wreck.

The question was solved as I rose and found a dozen or so soldiers advancing on me, weapons drawn. Curiosity would have to deal with it, since those weapons aimed at me were more immediately important.

"Good afternoon, gentlemen." A friendly smile formed on my lips. "Everything well?"

CHAPTER 54

✶

AN OFFER

The soldiers were unamused by my joke, but I was clearly no goblin, and Grandpa soon landed nearby. It seemed I'd actually lost him for a bit there, the plane not being quite as fast as the out-of-control train.

"You're absolutely sure you got them all?" a man in an officer's uniform repeated for what had to be the fifth time.

"I counted each one, and even looked for other survivors. We still need to pull whatever is left of their leader out of the wreckage though," I told him while pointing at the absolute mess that was the engine car. "Doubt there will be much, but you know, proper procedures and all that."

"Do not lecture me on procedure, boy. You may have endangered this whole operation with your actions."

"Actions which saved the lives of dozens of innocents."

"By risking the lives of many thousands more."

He had fairly little to say to me after that, but they did pull remains from the crash. There was little left, but skull fragments and a twisted, ruined corpse did show that we'd done it. We'd managed to actually kill the bastard.

Grandpa and I were held in place until nighttime, when a group of carriages arrived to take our plane, and us, to another location. We weren't locked in, but we were pretty well informed that this was only a courtesy, and that should we try to leave, their civility would be rescinded.

That was fine though. I was exhausted from all the fighting and sore from the injuries I'd taken. Now was as good a time as any to get a few hours in. After all, I might not be getting any decent sleep for some time after all this.

I finally awoke as dawn began its first attempt at cresting the horizon, pink and yellow light spreading through the sky. Grandpa was still awake, and looked quite rough. Apparently, he hadn't had the same thought and instead decided to stay up. When I attempted to ask him about it, he put a finger to his lips. Apparently, now was not the time for talking. I took a look outside and saw that we were back in some city, but I couldn't tell if it was the one we'd entered through the portal. Regardless, it certainly wasn't Exion. The streets here were a bit rougher, more winding, and the place just felt different. I could see an imposing wall in the distance, one of at least two visible to me, and they were marking off the outer edge of the metropolis. We were also on a hill. It was slight, but we were climbing ever upward.

We passed through yet another wall, and it made me wonder how many walls this place had. We seemed to now be entering a much richer district. Houses here were much larger, people better dressed, and the roads better maintained. It wasn't the stark difference between slums and impossible wealth, noticeably a nicer area.

The final wall we approached became clear as we grew nearer, and it surrounded one single residence. The castle was both a palace and a fortress—massive, with dozens of towers and parapets that rose to the heavens.

"Are we in the capital?" I asked.

"Yes, I suspect so," Grandpa replied, frowning. We could only be coming to this place to meet one person.

Once we were shown—forcibly escorted—to a meeting room it didn't take long for the king to meet us.

"I don't know if I should have you publicly flogged, thrown in prison, or given an award. Congratulations! It has been some time since that has happened," was his opener. We both stood before him in silence, letting him go on.

"Nothing to say for yourselves? Come now, you interfere in a military operation and nothing at all? Don't mistake me, I'm pleased that you managed to survive, and pleased that you killed those beasts while saving most of the people on that train, but sincerely, you could have said something first."

"Would you have authorized it?" I asked.

"No, of course not, but that's hardly the point. My auntie may have favored you, but this is beyond the pale."

"What would she have had me do?" I asked.

That particular question got me a look that would strip paint from walls.

"She'd have done it herself, but she was an order of magnitude more powerful and practiced than you." After schooling himself for a moment, His Majesty calmed himself. "Though that is a point."

"Nah, I met her when she was about his age. Well, quite a bit older actually—you lot age weird—but she gave the impression of being a little spitfire, regardless," said another voice. "Kind of reminds me of her in a way. Different sure, but still got that spark."

The man who'd interrupted us leaned against the wall beside the door. His hair was pure white and cropped short, a long flowing outfit, almost like a robe or coat over some comfy looking clothing, hung about him. His ears were pointed and long.

"Ambassador, I believe I requested you to remain behind," our ruler said through narrowed eyes.

My grandpa straightened visibly, eyes wide.

"Sit down," the newcomer said to Grandpa, and then he turned to the king. "And you did, but I couldn't bring myself to miss this. Moreover, I have a suggestion, if you lot are amenable."

"And what exactly would that be?" I asked.

"That you come work for me for a while, kid. I've got a couple jobs that need doing for my boss, and you seem just the right person for the job. Comes with free training and materials too."

"You don't have a boss," the king said flatly, as if it were obvious.

"Sure I do, and if you let me take the kid for a bit, I promise he'll be both punished and rewarded. The work I need done isn't easy, but if you can do it, you'll get much in return. So what do you all say?"

The man, who'd yet to introduce himself, stood there with a roguish grin, watching us. He'd not even told me what he wanted, or why me, but it seemed he thought I'd agree anyway. The older men in the room considered it, too, looking almost worried.

CHAPTER 55

EPILOGUE

Southern Elazia
A certain agent

People cheered as several ships returned to the harbor. The large military procession had been sent out only a few short weeks ago to test their might against the beasts of the ocean, and seeing them home brought no small smile to the faces of the people. Everyone knew that that ocean was the ultimate testing ground, and with so many ships they'd surely encountered battle.

I frowned when I saw them, one by one massive steel hulls parading in. They didn't bother to hide the damage they'd taken; though, it was clearly superficial, something to be fixed soon. Their cannons were massive, angled to fight any monster that came their way.

All of this was more buildup, more readying of military, but for what? Even those ships couldn't stand up to a powerful enough mage, and such people surely existed upon our shores. The people of Nicon knew it too. They knew that no matter what they had, other weapons and potent individuals would stop them from taking any of the major elven nations.

"Any rumors, old friend?" I asked as I slipped up next to a man I knew on the dock. He ran a bar nearby and had been coaxed out for the parade.

"Beautiful, isn't it? And yes, girlie, I have heard some things. These ships supposedly went to take care of some specific beasts. Heard a sailor talking about it," Scagan said with a smile. His name meant something like "water tree" in some ancient dialect.

"Oh? I do love hearing their stories. Could you introduce me?" I said with a false sweet smile.

"Still looking for a husband then? Surprising you've not succeeded. Heck, even a quick look tells how good your stock is," the older man said with a wink.

Of course he didn't know that what he saw was false—ears grown longer, facial structures altered just slightly, even a few markers added to my blood. It could fool any basic scan, as could my documents; though, it did come with drawbacks, painful ones.

"Mmm, wanna do it right," I told him. "Find the right one, you know?" It was good to make him think I was just as I presented myself—a bit of an airhead and a gossip of profound levels.

"Ah, I know, girlie, I know. Wish my daughters were as discerning sometimes. Itta's trying to court some man who I swear couldn't find his own feet."

"Haha, maybe I'll talk to her later then, if you want? So what are these for anyway? The navy going to clear out the sea? Because I doubt that will work, no matter how hard we try."

"Nah," he said, leaning in conspiratorially. "Same guy from before said he thought this was a practice run, see how good they are. I hear one of the human nations is all out of archmages. Fancy that, huh? The old monster they had fell over dead and nobody to replace her yet." He laughed. "We'll be going to show that filth who the real masters of the world are soon enough. Mark my words. Let the old folks up north see what we can do, reignite everyone's love for the Old Kingdom."

Fuck. If that was true, people needed to know, and now. The old monsters he spoke of, the pure elves who ruled like minor lords were not to be trifled with, and there was a good damn reason they didn't go attacking the humans. Well, several of them really, but two in particular that would absolutely come and bite us. I thought briefly about asking him more, but if I looked even the least bit disloyal... things could go very badly, and I wasn't sure I could get much else.

"Oh, how wonderful heroes make themselves in times like this." I bit my lip like some stupid girl dreaming of a strong husband and nothing else.

"Ha! A year or two more I think, at most. Think you can wait a bit longer?"

I scoffed. "Waiting is easy. Plenty of time," I said, nodding.

"Ah, but don't wait too long. No good comes of that," he chided.

"Mmm," I agreed.

Afterward, we sat and watched the ships roll by, and I tried to take the best notes I could of them. However, I was no expert in that kind of thing, and while I'd include the details I saw in my report home, I kind of doubted it would change much.

Goodbyes were shared, and we split. He returned to his patrons, and I returned to mine. Perhaps there was some way I could get backup, or someone could stop this foolishness before it exploded all over everyone's faces.

ABOUT THE AUTHOR

Wandering Agent is the North Carolina–based author of the Melody of Mana series as well as other fantasy and isekai stories.

JOIN THE FELLOWSHIP
follow us on our socials

 podiumentertainment.com

 @podiumentertainment

 /podiumentertainment

 @podium_ent

 @podiumentertainment

www.ingramcontent.com/pod-product-compliance
Lightning Source LLC
LaVergne TN
LVHW041914070526
838199LV00051BA/2616